Run With the Hunted 2:
Ctrl Alt Delete
Jennifer R. Donohue

I0456991

This is a work of fiction. Names, characters, places, and incidents either are the product of the author's imagination or are used fictitiously. Any resemblance to actual persons, living or dead, events, or locales is entirely coincidental.

Run with the Hunted 2 Ctrl Alt Delete © 2019 by Jennifer R. Donohue

Paperback ISBN: 978-1-945548-11-6
Ebook ISBN: 978-1-945548-10-9

For Jim

Chapter One

There's a dead pixel in the sky. Once I notice it, I can't ignore it. My eyes keep dragging up to look at it, no matter where I am or what I'm doing. It's an itch I can't scratch, a smear on the lens of my immersion. Plus, I don't know how long it's been there, and that bothers me.

The moon is always somewhere real-time appropriate. They tried the stars, in beta, but it took far too much bandwidth and nobody wanted a project like that. Now most places, it's flat black at night, sometimes cloudy. Just the moon. Sometimes a comet, if one is visible to the naked human eye real-time. It's ridiculous, what people bicker over when given the forum. Not a surprise. Just ridiculous.

So now that's my pet project. I spend my time adding stars. My personal night sky is a complete one, and when I have the time or the urge, I go through the old Hubble and Cassini and Kepler photographs, so if I want to spend time virtually lying on my back on a mountain or rooftop, just looking at all of the stars mankind had ever heard of, I can do that. I upload it to the public servers, little by little. My VR immersion rig is built from the best one money can buy, but the others are catching up. Managing the data better, with solid states and local nodes and the new fiber infrastructures.

I sometimes go to Carnivale in Venice at night time, since VR's the only place you can visit Venice anymore, the crenellated buildings all scanned and then rendered true to life, buildings which aren't standing in Venice anymore, sucked into the mucky lagoon or swallowed up by the waves or what have you. The twinkle lights, the gondolas. Everybody there is always all dressed up and masked. It adds another dimension, the party plus the game of IDing human or program. It isn't easy like it used to be. On impulse, I stop a man in a giraffe mask and, through my unicorn mask, ask "Do you see that in the sky?"

He looks down at me, and then up at the night sky, shakes his head. "See what?" he asks. He's human. I'm good at the Human or AI game. I'm not good at dealing with people in real life.

"Nevermind. Bug hunting." He nods and goes on his way. A SpaceX constellation shimmers by, reminding us all who we have to thank for worldwide internet.

My nose itches and I wrinkle it distractedly. Next would be to find somebody in the same VR node as me, using the same service provider. Theoretically. Except my VR node is just mine, paid for in an isolated jungle in Mexico, my rig built by hand piece by piece and hooked up to the local fiber after greasing appropriate political palms up the ladder, through intermediaries. Intermediaries are much better than me doing it. This could be real bad.

I move off the street, out of the crowd, and start my immersion exit protocol sequence to boot out of VR. It's been awhile, actually. Longer than a public protocol would've allowed. Public protocols existed for a reason, I'm happy to acknowledge that. But really they're unnecessary limits. Turns out, when you have the money for it, anything's possible.

The Carnivale around me fades away, the sounds and smells first, then the sights, like an old fashioned photograph un-developing, and I'm left temporarily with the flat gray haze of the non-waking state. It's drug induced, meant to be a body-brain buffer between the shock of VR immersion and consciousness, or vice versa. It isn't necessary if you're just upright using a VR headset. It isn't necessary if you're still just living your life.

Do I feel a needle sliding into my arm? I'm cotton-mouthed, not quite conscious, unable to protest. I like being more awake before the post-immersion wake-up meds.

After a moment, things come into sharper focus. The room's still dim, but ambient sounds return, the hum of servers and their water coolant, a compressor somewhere. Breathing, my own and somebody else's. The flat plastic smell of the carpet, still pretty new, mixed with the antiseptic smell of the medical equipment for VR immersion, the IV rig, all of that. The grass and gun oil smell of the intruder. I open my eyes slowly; eyelids tend to stick, especially after so long.

Dolly grins down at me. "Hey Bits," she says. "I wasn't sure tapping your machine with a hammer was the best way to get your attention, but I guess it got the job done. Hope I shot you up with the right stuff once that light turned green."

"Oh Jesus Christ, Dolly, what're you doing here?" I ask hoarsely. "And why didn't you just message me?"

"Well actually it's a good thing, 'cause it looks like you're here all by your lonesome. Empty IV bags aren't good for anybody." She drops a needle into the sharps container; it's really just B vitamins. I think.

"There's failsafes," I mutter, looking at the IV tree, but Dolly's right, those bags are empty. I rub my eyes. "How'd you even find me?"

"Oh you know. I got my ways," Dolly says, like that even means anything.

"Why'd you even find me?" I try.

"Well. I gotta find somebody."

"I'm not working right now, Dolly." I try to sit up, fail, and Dolly steadies me against the back of the cushy immersion chair.

"Yeah, Bits, I can see that. But I got something I need your help with. Lucky I actually know how to get you back on your feet."

"I'm starving." Starving not starving. I can't eat real food right away.

"You stink too. How long were you under?"

I reach for the data and it isn't there. "I don't...I don't know."

Dolly gives a low whistle. "Shit, Bitsy. Isn't that inadvisable in the extreme?"

"The benefits of having your own setup." I look around. The overhead light is out, burned out, because the one in the hall is on.

"Well let's get you hosed off and fed. Then I'll pull out my list."

"List. On paper." I rub my eyes again. They alternate between watering too much and not enough. This probably isn't the longest I've gone, but it feels like I was immersed for a long time. The chair massages muscles, mitigates some of the effects of immersion, but there's the sleepwalking stage of returning to real world consciousness, the inner ear disturbance of becoming upright again. Headaches, sometimes.

Dolly laughs. "I do everything I can on paper, Bitsy."

"Why didn't you just call Bristol?"

"Don't worry, this is in your wheelhouse." Her tone is off, I think. I can't tell. "Let's get you to the shower."

Chapter Two

Dolly's always been stronger than she looks. She supports me down the hall without breaking a sweat. I don't know how she's so strong, I could never carry her. She gets the shower running, locates shampoo, conditioner, pulls out towels and a bathrobe and smells them, shrugs. I remember my nose itched in VR, reach up to scratch it. My fingernails crackle with dry blood, but nothing hurts. Nosebleed maybe, mosquito maybe. "It seems like you've done this before, Dolly."

"Maybe I have. You steady enough to get yourself hosed off?"

"Yeah." I don't want Dolly to help me shower, that's not really where we are in our relationship.

"Alrighty. I'll look for your kitchen."

My stomach does a slow flop and I yawn to stem the nausea. "I'm sure that'll sound good when I'm more awake. Or in, like, two weeks." There's protocols. Vitamins. Meal replacements.

"It will." She pulls the door most of the way closed and walks off, whistling.

I drop my clothes on the floor, yoga pants and tank top, take a breath, and step into the spray. The water's too harsh at first, a thousand needles, and I stand off to the side, just letting it warm my skin.

Eventually I just go numb, and I fumble the bottles of shampoo and stuff. I'd buzzed my hair before I went under, and it's at a plush length that's soft and nice to touch. Eventually, or maybe it's quick, my fingertips go pruney, and I turn off the shower.

Going barefoot to the kitchen, every step feels new and tender. It doesn't really smell like cooking, but it doesn't smell like burning either. My nose just hasn't really kicked back on yet; sometimes my senses don't quite do what they're supposed to once I'm back in the real world. Takes some time to boot back up.

The coffee pot is steaming, almost full, and Dolly's head and shoulders in the refrigerator. "You still like your coffee sugar no milk, right? 'Cause your milk's way off."

"Right." She sets it in front of me, and the mug between my palms is far too warm at first, and I hold it gingerly on the butcher block countertop, perched on a stool.

"I don't know why you do that to yourself," Dolly says, watching me from the corners of her eyes. She's wearing her riot gear, I realize.

I shrug; it won't be a productive argument. "I thought you were gonna cook or something."

"Oh yeah. Gotta see if your eggs float first."

"If the eggs..."

"If they float, they're no good. If they don't, they're fine." Dolly gets out a glass bowl, slops some water in it, and slides the eggs from the carton in it. One of them floats, and she frowns and puts it back in the carton. The others don't, and she cracks them each, one-handed with surprising adroitness, into a skillet heating on the stove.

"Why are you in riot gear?" Should I be in riot gear?

"I told you." She glances at me, pokes the eggs. Did she? She could've. Time's skippy and gappy after a long immersion.

"I can't eat just regular food right away," I say. I can't decide if the eggs smell amazing or not. I can't decide if I'm amazed Dolly can cook or not.

"I know but you don't have any of that protein goo. Eggs are the best you've got here, buildin' blocks of life and all that. You don't even have the right vitamins in the cabinets, just some C. You should probably still take that." And Dolly loosens the lid and slides the plastic bottle across the butcher block.

"Didn't leave to get more after the last time," I say. Which seems like it is and isn't the right answer. I'm forgetting something and I have such a headache.

"That was dumb," Dolly says, back turned. The vitamin C goes down with effort, one of the pills sticking sideways a second, flooding my mouth with the sour almost-vomit taste. I drink more coffee, washing it away with the sweetbitter. I always have trouble swallowing vitamin C.

"It was."

"You get obsessed with that digital nonsense. Get too much in your head." Dolly slides a plate in front of me, then gets herself a cup of coffee. Sunny side up, the edges gone lacey from the heat. Golden tortillas, buttery. "Think you can keep any of that down?"

No. "I don't know yet."

"If you can't, don't push too hard. We'll get outta here tomorrow, next day, get you some protein slurries. Unless you got some squirreled away that you also forgot about."

"I don't know." When did I last have to say I don't know so many times? I shake my head, but that's a mistake, as the world around me tilts, shifts, rights itself. "Where are we going? Why are you here, anyway?"

"We're headin' to California first," she says around a mouthful of tortilla and egg, some yolk running down her chin. "Anyway why'd you pick Mexico?"

"The climate and the exchange rate."

"Climate's nice, you're right about that." Dolly's already done eating. I look down at my plate, at the glistening eggs, think about how the yolk will slump out when I puncture it with a fork, and I burp a sour, vitamin C tasting burp. I shove my plate at Dolly. "You sure?"

"Yeah, I'm sure. And it hurts worse to throw up when you're empty."

"I wouldn't know." Dolly tucks into that plate with equal gusto, then gets up for more coffee.

I try again. "Dolly, why are you here?"

"I told you, something we gotta get done. It's kind of urgent, but I don't know the timeline."

Just perfect. "And I told you I wasn't working."

"Yeah, are we gonna sit around repeating ourselves, or are we gonna talk like grownups?" She pushes away her second empty plate. "You care if I smoke?"

"No. Or, I don't know yet."

"Fair enough." Dolly slaps her pockets until she pulls out a pack of cigarettes, cheap plastic lighter tucked into the wrapper, pulls one out, lights it. The smell of tobacco is sort of soothing, actually. Makes me think of...somebody. My father? My memories have a way of being scrambled, especially after time in full tactile VR immersion. It's expected. Dolly is being uncommonly patient, actually. Though doesn't she normally smoke ecigs? Not this much, though. Not one after the other, constantly.

"So what's the job, Dolly? What's the plan?" It's amazing Dolly hasn't already launched into it, pouring out the salt shaker and drawing diagrams on the butcher block with her fingertip, leaving the cigarette just kind of stuck there in the corner of her mouth.

"We have a friend in a tight spot. Need to bust her out."

"Out of where? A prison, I assume, from the way you're saying it."

"Something like that."

"So a black site then."

"Maybe? Once we know where she is it'll be easier."

"Stateside? Mexico? Elsewhere?"

"I'm. Um. Not sure." Dolly drags at the cigarette, not looking at me. I'm used to Dolly being rock solid. Evasive isn't unusual, we're all pretty shaky on the concept of honesty. But there's something else there that I can't track, under the usual Dolly brashness.

"What do you mean you're not sure?" I get myself up this time, to pour more coffee in on the sugar sludge in the bottom of my mug. The ring of my spoon against the porcelain is very sharp. I feel like I'm not really seeing in color right now, everything infinite shades of gray.

"It's probably stateside. We were supposed to rendezvous. When that didn't happen, I poked around, reached some dead ends. Drew my logical conclusions."

"Then came here."

"More or less."

"No, you said you went to Bristol first."

"Did I?" Dolly is quiet for a long time, jiggling one leg, smoking. She did, didn't she?

"So what, then?"

"Well. I need you to do some tracking, first off."

I sigh. "The easiest way to do that is reimmersion." That's inadvisable. If Dolly even knows that. She know weapons, that's for damn sure. Cars. Geography, military protocols, including, evidently, some VR immersion ones, but not enough to lecture me.

"Good thing we didn't leave yet," Dolly says with a crooked grin, getting up and running her cigarette butt under the faucet. She comes and collects the plates, washes them, half whistling that same tune that I don't recognize. She does that a lot sometimes.

Chapter Three

Despite Dolly's rush, she doesn't let me re-immerse right away. I totter around my dim abandoned estate on tender-soled feet, Dolly smoking almost constantly and hovering at my elbow. The floor's all tiles, polished coral, no carpeting. Most of the windows are shuttered, so it's cooler in the house, even though the only room with actual environmental controls is the VR room, for the rig and medical stuff. When we step out into the courtyard, it's like stepping into a mouth. The jungle, evening closing around us, is close and damp. Birds I don't know the names of make their strange cries in the trees.

"The locals here don't put worms in their tequila," I say to Dolly.

"No?"

"No, they put a scorpion in each bottle. It makes me think of Macbeth."

"Why's that?" Dolly lights another cigarette.

"Everybody talks about Lady Macbeth's mad scene, out damn spot, but Macbeth has his own mad scene too. He says at one point, my mind is full of scorpions."

"I like Shakespeare," Dolly says.

"You do?"

"I guess mostly the fighting. Shakespeare's bloody." She laughs and drags on her cigarette. "You're sure you're okay to do this? You don't wanna sleep?"

"It's okay. You said it was probably urgent, I';; go back into immersion."

"If you're sure." Dolly shifts uneasily, gun belt creaking. "I don't want to push you past—"

"It's okay. You asked, I'll do it." Maybe then she'll leave me alone. Probably not.

I REMEMBER DOLLY SAYING something about taking a hammer to the rig, and pause to examine the machines. There's a ding in the casing of one, a hammer lying on top. I pick it up, hold it a minute to gauge my strength. Since my immersion chair is the best money can buy, I've hardly lost any muscle mass.

"Dolly, seriously?"

"Like I said, I didn't know your wakeup protocols and it seemed like the fastest way. Was I wrong?"

"Not exactly. Better than unplugging me I guess."

"Which would do what, anyway?"

"Probably nothing. I assume I'd wake up eventually."

"See, it's that assume word. We don't like that assume word."

"It's like how in the olden days you used to wait for your computer to tell you it was safe to turn off. Or you used to manually eject a drive. It probably wasn't necessary, but better safe than sorry, right?"

"I know they don't think it's safe to immerse for six months."

"Another reason I came here. People were more likely to leave me alone, between the cartels and the tigers."

"Are you talking about the riddle, or literal tigers?"

"The real estate agent seemed worried about literal tigers. I haven't seen any."

"Christ, Bits." Dolly stares at me, frowning.

"What, did we finally find something you're afraid of?"

"Nah, I just wouldn't've left the AK in the Jeep if I thought there were tigers. Gimme a sec."

"I can't believe they still make those," I say when she comes back.

"This particular one is a more recent knockoff," Dolly says, leaning it up. "Hard to argue with a workhorse like that. I mean, there's more modern analogs, caseless, ammunition AR overlay, all that good stuff. But, can't hack an AK with one of your VR dealies. And you can't pull an AR enabled firearm out of a puddle and still expect it to work right, so there's that."

"There's that," I agree. "Though there are some waterproof AR weapons."

"Yeah, but they're not AKs."

"You can't convince me you have brand loyalty."

"I don't. Lots of folks do, but I wonder if it's more superstition, like using the same shoelaces all the time."

"You don't use anything all the time. You don't even care what kind of cigarettes you smoke."

"Exactly." Dolly grins.

"So you're...reverse superstitious?"

"Anti-superstitious? Whatever. This isn't a movie; no sense only using a rifle you named or some stupid shit like that, right?"

"Right." I settle back into the VR chair, pull the helmet down over my head, feeling the wires spider into place through my hair. A shaved head isn't necessary, I just like doing it, especially before a long immersion. "So who am I looking for?"

Dolly hesitates. Dolly never hesitates. "Bristol."

I jerk upright, the wires scrabble-tightening in my hair. "What? What do you mean Bristol? What happened? Why did you take so long to tell me?"

"Shh, shh now, calm down. You're all fucked up, you needed time. Even this is pushing it, but I dunno how long we can wait anymore."

"Why isn't she in Morocco?"

"Well that's a million dollar question, right?"

"Dolly." I was ready to be sick before we ever started this conversation and now I close my eyes, clench my jaw.

"I know, I know, I'm sorry."

I take a deep slow breath, let it out. "Okay. I can't just search the internet at large for Bristol, especially not after the scrubbing work I've put in. Give me a waypoint."

"Well I think it's likely that the county sheriff in Montana who arrested her has probably contacted DHS by now."

"Homeland. Of course." And of course I can't say no. And of course...I want the challenge. Hacking Homeland. "What the fuck *happened*?"

"Well I think she thought getting caught by as small a fish as possible would keep the big fish away the longest."

"Yeah but—" I have too many questions and they bottle-neck where my thoughts meet my voice, so nothing comes out.

"Time's wasting, Bitsy. Come on, run me through your protocols."

I show her on the console what to hit to cue my logoff sequence. I can do it myself anytime I want, but emergencies are emergencies. Then I close my eyes and start my login sequence. I wonder for a sec if maybe it won't work, if I'm too saturated or too agitated and the autohypnosis will just fizzle, leave me awake and in the real world with my scalp tingling. The brain-computer interface implant can only do so much sometimes.

I open my eyes in Texas. Or at least the official Virtual Reality architecture of Texas, the Lone Star State. The DHS mainframe is in Texas, I guess in what used to be army property, and army buildings almost always look the same. To me, anyway.

There's regulation height chain link fence, with razorwire along the top of it, and what looks like people in uniforms, patrolling with dogs in bulletproof vests. It seems particularly mean to shoot a dog. It seems sadistic to do it in Virtual Reality. What, you want to know if they programmed authentic dog in pain noises?

I stroll up to the gates, fiddle with the lock. People make a big deal when they refer to something as military grade, but in my experience it tends to mean the same quality as everything else, if not slightly under. It just costs more. It isn't actually coded better, and I'm in without any trouble. Nobody notices. The patrolling 'personnel' are automated anti intrusion systems, not in-person, VR immersed hackers. Or whatever the alphabet soup government calls them. Tiger teams, that's the old fashioned term. Maybe they still use it. It's the on old fashioned thing I like, the vocabulary from the first days of the internet.

Everything's neatly labeled and with clear direction, that's a military grade truism, and plain old records is as good a place to start as any. I flip to subheading DHS arrests, sorted by most recent. There's a file for supply rig hijacking with inventory from the rig, but the numbers just kind of swim in my brain and I shake it off. Too much, and not Bristol. They raided people ordering pressure cookers. Deportation targets. I look at the date and can't make sense of it, if it's sooner or later than I think it should be. I shuffle through to subheading prisoner holdings. Subheading prisoner transfers. Run her aliases. If a small-time sheriff arrested her and transferred her up the chain, county to state to federal...Bristol, Madison, Chelsea, Florence, Paris, Devon, and we have a winner. She's somewhere in Kansas, transferred from locals in Montana. And not for long.

I look up. The records section is coded to look like an old fashioned storage room, metal shelving, cardboard boxes, signs on the walls. Or maybe all records storage rooms still look like this in person, if they're kept analog. We've all seen pictures of the National Tracing Center. But the signs on the walls are different now from when I got here. Glowing? Did they change color? I head for the exit, thinking about those coded German shepherds in their bullet proof vests. I don't know if the color shift means a change in threat awareness level, but I've got what I came for.

Technically, I can exit immersion from the facility, but exiting from free space is preferable. Technically. So far as protocols go. Because I follow protocols so closely. The door behind me opens and I freeze in place, the copy transfer of Bristol's file ticking off its last bit of percentage. There's a member of personnel in the space here, and I'm not keen to find out how DHS counters hackers. You hear horror stories, of course. Recursive hypnotic viruses that leave people fucked up so you can't think can't sleep can't—

"Excuse me, ma'am, I'm going to need to see your credentials," a voice says, close. Shit.

"Of course, of course," I mutter, initiating my countdown, fumbling as though I have lag and my security packet is on the way, 3-2-1, golf-tango-echo—no, no that's wrong and then I'm shaken up, distracted, and can't restart the protocol, fuck.

"Your credentials," the voice repeats, and then I'm facing another woman of similar height and build, if our avatars are at all representative of our real selves. "Or we're going to have a problem."

"You seem to be suggesting we don't already. What's your rank?"

"Corporal."

"Well, Corporal, are you in the habit of accosting everybody who enters the records room?" I ask, abandoning the exit protocol for the moment, shifting rapidly through my falsified credentials. I skimmed a sergeant's last year, year before, when me and Dolly and Bristol had the business with the diamonds, because you just never know when having officer credentials will come in handy, even cross agency.

"Considering it's my job, yes, yes I am. It's protocol to ask for credentials, for credentials to be presented, for the handshake, and for parties to be on their way. I apologize that this seems to be a foreign concept for you—" the Corporal is struggling to capture my attention, to trap me in the immersion, backtraces already running, for all the good it'll do her. My signal reroutes all over the place.

"Sergeant," I say with a certain amount of smugness, presenting the credentials, real ones cobbled together with updates and enough of my own bioreadings to make it that much more authentic and confusing.

"Sergeant," the Corporal repeats, sounding mystified. She scans the credentials, and steps back.

"Everything is in order then, Corporal?" I ask.

"Yes, ma'am. You understand that I—"

"Yes I do, Corporal. There's no need for this incident to go any further. Just doing your due diligence. So few people do more than lip service anymore," I say. The exit door is so close.

"Thank you, ma'am. Have a good day."

"You too, Corporal." We salute each other, and I feel ridiculous, and she fades back into the code of the records room. I leave out the exit door, go down a featureless hallway that makes me wonder why the fuck somebody coded it, and then I'm back under the VR Texas sky again, once again at the end of my immersion exit protocol, 3-2-1, golf, tango, foxtrot, oscar, and then I'm sitting up in my rig in Mexico, tearing the headset off and saying to wide-eyed Dolly "Pull the plug and get the hammer."

"What?"

"Did I stutter? Pull the plug and get the hammer." My immersion exit is short, precious seconds trimmed away, hacked off, until it's that little packaged phrase, tricking my brain into waking up in my body again instead of in the machine. If that Corporal in Texas decides she's not so sure of me after all, she's sending a red alert directing resources at locating my signal. But it's ridiculous to be so worried about that, I'm so careful. Tracing me would take literally hours, I'm sure of it. But still.

"You're the boss," Dolly says with a shrug and a curious grin. She sticks a cigarette to her lip and lights it as she leaves the room. I turn sideways in the chair and belch sourly. My stomach doesn't seem like it's moored properly.

By the time Dolly's back with the hammer, I've recovered enough to pull the plugs on all of the VR gear, pull the hard drives on what I'm keeping and bag them, jam them into carrying cases. I always have to be prepared for these eventualities, though I don't remember who taught me that. I remember the smell of cigarette smoke, or is it gunfire? Pain spikes in my temples and I make a mental note to chase those thoughts later.

"You're sure you want to do this?" Dolly asks.

"Sure. I don't expect unmarked helicopters in the next twelve hours or anything, but better safe than sorry, right? Another wakeup, and we're blowing town, you already said."

"I didn't know if you'd need more time. I've never seen you in such bad shape."

"Not many people have." We let that hang for a minute there between us. Really, I'm not sure if I've ever seen myself in such bad shape either. "Okay I packed what I need. Everything's unplugged, but that doesn't mean some things don't still have juice. Be careful."

"So that means you got it, you found her."

"Yeah, yeah, Bristol's in Kansas right now."

"Right now?" Dolly is kind of swinging the hammer in her right hand; there's something about a hammer that makes you want to swing it.

"There's an interrogation team coming in four days, and she'll be moved after that, but they didn't have a point B. So, that could mean a lot of things. Release amongst them, I guess."

"That's our Bits always seeing the silver lining," Dolly says, in the least silver lining voice I've ever heard, and then she hits the VR immersion rig with the hammer. I imagine she does it as hard as she can, judging from the scream of metal and how far some of the shards go.

Chapter Four

"Fucking Kansas," Dolly says, an hour later on the veranda.

"I'm sure Kansas has nice things going for it," I say, sipping my protein slushy. Mangosteen, a fruit the Queen of England once offered a hefty sum for, delivered fresh from Asia. I read that on the inside of a vintage Snapple lid.

"Yeah, sure. They probably wind farm the hell out of it. Isn't that where a lot of astronauts came from?"

"That's Ohio."

"Really, do you know my main problem is with her being in Kansas?"

"No, Dolly, tell me."

"It's so flat." I just look at her. I should know why she thinks that's bad. I used to know why she thinks that's bad. "It's flat. It's hard to insert on a military facility anyway, but a flat one? They see you on approach. They see you coming thirty miles away. It's terrible."

"Then we hijack the transport."

"If there is transport and they aren't just gonna put a bullet in the back of her head in the basement."

I've never seen Dolly this kind of agitated. Not even during the diamond thing, when we thought maybe both the American and Russian governments were after us for scary Cold

War nuclear codes. No, Dolly was still her grinning fucked up, southern belle, devil-may-care self. I should feel more amped up, but everything is muffled, distant.

"Well, step one, we get back stateside," I say. "We hook up with people you know or people I know. DHS'll think she's too valuable to just execute. Or, they won't know what they have and just shuffle her around."

"Yeah. Maybe." Dolly stands at the edge of the veranda, looking out across the courtyard towards the jungle. "I almost wish we would see a tiger," she says.

"I know what you mean."

"I heard someplace that a tiger won't attack you if you're looking at it. So people in jungles where there's tigers, sometimes they wear masks on the backs of their heads, so they've got faces there too."

"I didn't know that."

"Makes you wonder why something that big and deadly is worried about you just looking at it."

"It kind of does." Maybe tigers are just lazy.

Dolly lights another cigarette, still looking at the jungle. Her AK is slung on its web harness, barrel against her leg. She always looks most at home when she can open carry.

"Of course, breaking into a federal clink is crazy," Dolly says. I blink at her. Time passed somehow. She doesn't have a cigarette anymore and it's raining.

"Yes, it is. But crazy never stops you from doing anything."

"You know me so well."

"We just need to get there and then we'll see how to do it." I normally want far more of a plan than this. Contingencies.

Alternate approaches. This isn't even a plan. We normally want more than a plan.

"True enough." She's quiet for a minute. "Anything we can do to get you tuned in faster?"

"No. Unfortunately my implant doesn't have any kind of fast acclimation programming. It was on my list." I could tinker with the implant, maybe. If the problem is the implant. "Something to work on on the road, maybe."

"Yeah, maybe. Funny, the things the brain can do, ain't it?"

"Yeah, funny."

"Not, like funny ha ha."

"What you think to laugh at and what I do aren't always the same thing."

"Isn't that the truth. You hungry yet?"

"No, I'm not hungry yet, you bottomless pit. You can eat if you want. I'm just going to sit out here and wait for tigers."

"Fair enough. Holler if you need me."

"I will."

Dolly clomps inside, untied boot laces clattering on the tile floors. She's whistling again. I hold my phone in my lap, but I don't feel the impulse to fiddle with it just yet. I should. There's so much to look up. The borders, if anything's going to affect our crossing, Nebraska. But I just stare off into the jungle, listening to the slowly pattering rain, which also sounds just like the wind through the leaf laden branches, except there isn't any wind, just the rain. I shake my head. That kind of circular thinking is too easy to get trapped in when you immerse in VR a lot, and especially right now. I set the tablet on one of the little end tables and walk out into the courtyard, the gravel prickling the soles of my feet, the rain pattering onto the crown of my head, my shoulders, my arms, trickling warm down my skin like sweat I didn't work to shed. I tilt my head back and let the rain fall like tears on my face, and maybe I'm crying. I should be crying, I'm so goddamn scared for Bristol, I know this intellectually, but even so, I can't really react.

I go back inside before I'm soaked, trailing my fingers along the walls until I stop in front of one of the few decorations I added, an ugly painting of an old fashioned English hunting scene. Men in red coats and white breeches on horseback, hounds coursing, a fox running. I reach up and lift it off the wall, heavy in its dark wood frame, and it slips out of my hands, drops straight to the floor. The red coats seem very bright, throbbing off the painting, but nothing else does. Dolly appears near me, impossibly fast. "You okay?"

"Yeah. Gonna need money, right?" I nod at the wall safe that the painting covered.

"I guess?" From the look on her face, she looked for it and didn't pick the right spot.

I spin the dial, left right left, then press my palm to the biometric scan, where it tingles for thirty seconds, and then beeps and hisses open. I've got a variety of currencies. Bundled U.S. dollars, rolls of gold coins that a number of countries will take, and the keychain authenticator for one of my offshore bank accounts.

"We need to keep this small, I don't know where you have people you trust." Or where I do. Lockhart's still okay but not near Kansas.

"I admit I was probably jumping to conclusions when I said they'd probably just shoot her."

"Probably." I don't like talking about this. "They don't seem to know who she is yet. They don't know about the diamond business. But they must think she knows something they want to know, and they must have a reason to have her mobile." Back when we first got together, started doing jobs, I hacked agencies one by one and erased things in our digital records. Fingerprints. DNA from cheek swabs. I altered descriptions and overwrote pictures and voice and video. It isn't impossible to connect dots across the years and make a case regarding who each of us is, the internet is forever after all, but I did my damndest to make it as impossible as possible.

"They always think somebody knows something. Do you want another smoothie?"

"No, I don't want another smoothie. You're taking very good care of me, Dolly but right now I want to know a little bit about how we're going cowboy rebel against the United States Goddamn Department of Homeland Security to cut Bristol loose of whatever it is you got yourselves into."

"Well we had a job," she says, and then my head fills with static. When it clears, I'm sitting on a wooden stool in the bathroom, lights bright white, too bright, Dolly still talking and the electric razor humming over the sides of my head. It's how I prefer it, rather than the allover shave, though I've walked around with both.

"Thanks," I say to Dolly. A cigarette burns on the edge of the sink.

"You're welcome. You're all in and out, is that normal?"

Negative. "It'll pass."

"I know it will. But you've got a long time to make up for."

"You keep saying that. It isn't the longest I've gone."

"Isn't it? And what's the longest you've gone?"

Was it a year? "I can't remember."

"Do you remember anything I just told you?"

"You and Bristol were doing a job."

She frowns, reaches to pick up the cigarette, take a drag. "No. *We* had a job. All three of us."

So after we separated in Berlin. After Bristol went to Morocco and I came here and Dolly went...wherever it was Dolly went. "And whatever we did got Homeland on us."

"You don't remember?" She's watching me in the mirror, razor silent, loose hair scratchy on my neck.

I try. But reaching for the memories is like trying to get a piece of eggshell out of cake batter; I think I have it and it slips away, again and again. "I don't remember," I say, and I realize I'm breathing a little too hard, sweating a little. "Something went wrong though."

"Take it easy. Yeah, yeah it did." She takes another short, hard drag on the cigarette, puts it out in the sink. "And if I try to tell you again, you're just gonna reboot again. Which is pretty freaky, gotta say."

"Try living it." I've never had it this bad. Sometimes it's just how the real world is, a little bit here and there. Glitches like everything's digital. Time speeds up or slows down and you miss things or you see everything, more than is humanly possible. I had to have been counterhacked. Something in my equipment got screwed up, and I didn't know, and it was wrong for months. I immersed like that. Who knows what I did, what it did to me. No wonder I didn't recognize the date.

Chapter Five

The border crossing into California is no sweat, Dolly says. I don't remember it. Evidently we stopped at some point and put our questionable gear in the box. I probably would have worried more about it, if I could have gotten my thoughts to focus on it at all. Instead, I keep looking at the ocean, once we can see the ocean, and I think about the plans the military had to train and weaponize dolphins. Or had the military actually accomplished that? There was that super weird experiment in like, the 1970s with the partially flooded house that the woman lived in with the male dolphin, but that was more of a communications experiment than a weapons one, which was weird too, because it seems to me that we actually did establish a good interspecies communication. Maybe it was more like the 1990s that they were using dolphins to defuse bombs, or that they were putting lasers on them or whatever. Dolphin codebreakers. I can't help myself and giggle.

"What's, uh, what's goin' on Bitsy?" Dolly asks. It's dark out and we've just pulled into a hotel parking lot. It looks like...oh what was that movie, with the murders?

"Just tired and thinking about things. I'm sorry."

"Well, I'm toast. You're okay with sharing a room, I assume."

"Yeah, though you throw elbows in your sleep," I say.

"Yup, separate beds," Dolly says. "Sit tight, I'll talk to the friendly front desk clerk."

Hope he doesn't want to murder us, I think. Though honestly, any desk clerk that breaks into a room with the two of us would get more than they bargained for. Well, that breaks into a room with Dolly. But Dolly is more than a handful for most people. Meaner than a rattlesnake, when she wants to be. I don't know where I learned that saying; probably from Dolly herself.

"Bitsy, come on," Dolly says, and I get the sense she's been repeating herself for awhile. She's being far more patient than I thought she had in her.

"Sorry. I didn't think you'd be so fast."

"It's okay. You can get that bag, at least? I'll grab the duffles."

"I can carry my duffle," I protest, mostly because she expects me to.

"It's not a big deal. Come on."

We walk across the parking lot and I realize about halfway across that it isn't gravel or dirt, but shells. Oysters maybe or clams, or maybe just whatever got dredged up. Maybe it's sand dollars and it wrecked the mermaid economy for that decade, plunged them into a Depression. I stifle what I just know would be a crazy kind of giggle. Dolly's worried enough already.

"What did the room set you back?" I ask as Dolly unlocks it with a key, not a keycard. It has an oblong plastic keychain with the number on it in black letters.

"Don't worry about it. Not like I don't got the money."

"You didn't blow it all on guns, booze, and muscle cars?"

"I did not."

"Dolly. I might be disappointed. Maybe a racehorse?"

"Negative." Dolly pops the snap on her handgun and goes rapidly into the room, flicking the lights on, checking the corners. It's clear and seems clean enough, the carpet and comforters smelling of cleaner and detergent, a faint amount of sand squeaking under Dolly's combat boots on the bathroom tiles.

"Well if you didn't blow all your money then why were we doing a job?"

""Some things in life, I do for the thrill of them, Bits. Or because I feel like I have to. You got anything like that?" Dolly asks, with her knife's edge smile.

"I guess I do," I say. "Bristol though?"

"If nothing else, we're thick as thieves. As the saying goes." Dolly says, sitting on the end of her bed and untying her boots. "You hungry?"

"Not yet. Order what you want."

"I hope you don't mind, I stole the blender from your hacienda, and brought a cooler full of protein, so we've got you covered."

"Why would I mind?"

"I dunno. I've just always been one of those ask forgiveness, not permission kind of people."

"I'm surprised you didn't bring more of the food, honestly."

"Didn't see the logistics of it, honestly, all that raw meat. The tigers'll get it. Or somebody else'll get wise to the fact that you've cleared out and head up there. Whichever."

"News travels fast," I say.

Dolly paws through the nightstand, then turns on the AR TV and looks up local delivery on the internet. "Thai, Mexican, Ethiopian, Chinese, Taiwanese, Japanese, Korean, Indian, Cajun, Jamaican, Nova Scotian, French—"

"Nova Scotian?" I ask.

"Yeah. Looks like mostly seafood?"

"You know you really just want tacos to go with the tequila you brought. Going through the choices is for funzies."

Dolly laughs. "I do. But maybe I was hoping something would catch your fancy."

"Just get the damn tacos, Dolly."

"I'm getting the damn tacos. Geeze you're pushy."

I lie back on the other bed. "*I'm* pushy," I say to the ceiling. I think about the VR headset in my bag. The AR contact lenses.

"Yup, pushy and a chatterbox. Just always runnin' your mouth, Bits, it's real hard for anybody else to get a word in edgewise." Dolly is flipping through the channels at a rapid pace, almost faster than I can really follow. Spy movie, car race, weather, politics, home renovations, golf, game show, war movie...

"Well I'll just have to work on that, Dolly. I'm glad you brought it to my attention."

"Hey, we're all works in progress, right?"

"I guess." Dolly stops on some music channel. Ten hours in the car and I still feel like I'm moving, stationary on the bed. That two-lane highway that headed north from Mexico is well kept but hard traveled, so it doesn't exactly maintain a glassy fresh-paved condition. There are some roads, all over the world but I think at least one in California, that if you drive in a certain lane at a certain speed, the asphalt is grooved in such a way that the tires passing over them played a song. I fell down that YouTube rabbit hole once, and during one of my immersions went all over the place to many of those locations and drove over them, in an electric sports car with the top down, the wind through my hair. I didn't visit the California one, though.

The tacos come and Dolly pays, her boot laces rattling against the legs of all the furniture in the room. I think maybe I'll just melt into the bed, my limbs so leaden, my eyelids feeling like those bibs they put on you in the dentist's office. Dolly runs the chain and the bolt on the door, and then sets the rustling paper delivery bags down somewhere. She's still for a moment, then comes and pulls my boots off and drops them on the floor, and I slip into a sleep that feels dreamless but isn't, not quite. It's just filled with a view of looking through the windshield at the highway through my new sunglasses as we drove north under a blue sky.

Chapter Six

"We need to call somebody," Dolly says in the morning. "We aren't gonna take a transport just the two of us, much as I'd like to be that badass."

"It'd be a good story," I say. The coffee maker is going and Dolly's eating a cold taco, watching the news in not-English.

"Atta girl." Dolly grins and balls up her taco paper, gets up to pour coffee. "How you feeling?"

"I don't know."

She hands me a mug and I slide my sunglasses on, take a sip. Dolly put the magical just right amount of sugar into the coffee. On the news, some celebrities are doing...something. Some world leaders are going...somewhere. I can't remember right this second who the president of anywhere is. "I think Nicky is the pony to bet on."

"Nicky...Nicolai, the guy we met in Paris? Your Russian friend?"

"The one and the same. He happened to be...well, I won't say in town, we ain't in a town. In the general vicinity. And he might know some people we can pick up along the way, get a temporary crew rolling."

Nicolai is one of those citizen of the world looking types, and you can't quite nail him down until he opens his mouth and you heard the Russian in his voice. Well, Bristol nailed him down, when we met him in Europe, but apparently she'd spent some time in Moscow because of course she did. He has a good tan, but that could mean he has a natural tan or he likes tanning or he got genetically modded to look like that.

"I brought you girls some vodka," he says, when he shows up. He kisses us each on the cheeks, me first and fast before I even realize that's what he's doing, Dolly slower.

"And we've got tequila with a scorpion in it, so if you wanna swap, we can do that," Dolly says, lighting a cigarette and offering him the pack. He looks at it, and makes a face, shaking his head.

"Dolly, you'll excuse me for saying you have no taste."

"I will. I have no taste on purpose. If it doesn't matter what I'm smoking, it means I can always get a pack of cigarettes I'm happy with."

"While that's perfectly defensible, it also prevents you from taking joy in the things you like," Nicolai says, pulling out his own pack of cigarettes. He looks at me right as I take a bite out of a coffee wafer candy bar. "She gives this same explanation for beer, and everything else."

"Except guns," I say with my mouth full. Eating candy doesn't feel like real eating.

"Except guns," he agrees. "Dolly has the most snobbish taste possible in guns and ammunition."

"Does that make up for it?" Dolly asks.

"It makes you a pain in the ass, my friend."

Dolly laughs. "I've been told that more than once."

"I can imagine," Nicolai says. "Now what's the job?"

"We need a few operators to hit a convoy and extract a very good friend of mine. Ours." Dolly says, smoothly, without batting an eye. She must've practiced in her head.

"Sounds like a good time," Nicolai says. "When will this party begin?"

"Couple days. In Kansas."

"A state I've never seen." He shrugs

Dolly grins, plops into one of the wooden chairs by the little table. "Interested in attendin' the party, are you?"

"Only if somebody else can bring the beer. Honestly, she drinks swill," he says to me despairingly, and I can't help but laugh. "What's your part in this?"

"The same as in Paris. Equipment and communications." I remember Paris, at least. It was before the diamonds.

"I'm happy to hear that."

"Thanks." I finish my candy bar. Paris was easy. No shots fired, hardly any blood pressures raised, everything just smooth sailing, smooth talking. Who was the other person working with us in Paris? I can't remember. Somebody Bristol knows, a woman from South Africa or Zaire, who split her time between there and Paris.

"So you know some folks then?" Dolly asks.

"I can make some calls. I know some people who might be on board."

Dolly blows a smoke ring. "If they're not?"

"I know other people, in Detroit, if the first group doesn't work out."

"It's DHS. Probably a small group, definitely covert."

"You do get into the most interesting difficulties, Dolly," Nicolai says, and I wonder what their history is.

"You still in?" she asks, still smiling, but her eyes narrow just a little, watching him. Her cigarette is in her left hand, her right hand resting on her stomach as she slouches back in her chair. It's no coincidence that her pistol is holstered there on her left, unsnapped. And if I noticed that, Nicolai has to see it too.

Nicolai smiles and drags on his cigarette, his posture changing not at all. "What do I care, if it's DHS? They aren't omnipotent, they can't track us to the ends of the earth. Especially not with Bits on comms and equipment. Especially if they're keeping it quiet."

"You know what to look forward to, if we get collared," Dolly says.

"That's the risk people like us take, with the life we lead," he says with a shrug. "I'll call my people. They'll want to be paid."

"They'll be paid," Dolly says evenly, stubbing out her cigarette in the clamshell ashtray.

Chapter Seven

Dolly goes out to get cigarettes and something for dinner. She does not say what she is purchasing in either of those categories. Nicolai goes for beer and then occupies himself with phone call after phone call, walking up and down the entire sidewalk in front of the motel, talking and smoking and occasionally gesticulating. The front desk clerk look out the window at him a couple of times, and I message Dolly to remind her to go over and pay for adding a guest to our room or whatever.

I put in my AR contacts, and then I get the blender out of the Jeep and make one of my smoothies. I drink it in a chair on the sidewalk outside of our room while looking at the glimmer of the ocean across the highway and across a further expanse of beach. I look at the passing cars, their flickering broadcasts. I glance at Nicolai when he comes past but I leave my phone in my pocket. His calls aren't my business. I can do it with just my implant and contacts, sometimes, but no. I might be starting to feel something like hungry. Maybe. It's still hard to tell. Some kids come by on skateboards, yelling to each other and using the parking lot railings as something to do tricks off of for awhile, and I watch until I suck bottom on the smoothie.

Dolly pulls into the parking lot right as Nicolai hangs up his fifth or sixth phone call, and carries a cardboard box full of takeout boxes.

"What'd you get to eat?" I ask.

"Somali. Peanut chicken, among other things."

"Sounds good," I say.

"You bitch about things I pick out and then bring back Red Stripe," Dolly says thoughtfully, popping the top off one on her forearm. Dolly is a source of many of those sorts of tricks.

"I like Red Stripe," Nicolai says, looking at me in appeal.

"If you get Red Stripe actually in Jamaica, you get the recycled bottles, so the glass is all dinged up," I say. "They send the fresh bottles out of country."

"I didn't know you ever went to Jamaica, Bits," Dolly says. I can't really tell what her tone of voice is.

"I've been to a lot of places," I say. "With and without you and Bristol." In person and in VR. I went to Jamaica, not long after the diamonds. I went to a lot of places, various banks, Jamaica, Cape Town, Hong Kong, Berlin, all over the place, put money and data caches in safety deposit boxes, so if I can get to a place, I'll always have means.

I remember sitting under the umbrella at my hotel in Jamaica, trying to figure out what color blue I'd call what they painted the little individual cabin roofs, almost like it was one of those Greek islands with the white buildings. They used copper to make that blue, had always made it like that, maybe since the Renaissance. I remember ordering Red Stripe because I'd heard of it but also because it was local, because it had a color in its name.

"Bitsy, come back to us," Dolly says with her signature grin, Titanium White. They probably aren't her original teeth. Not a whole lot of people necessarily have their original parts, in this world of tomorrow, with cybernetic organs, lenses for eyes, prosthetics. Teeth are a logical progression, considering how few insurance companies, for however few people had insurance, actually offered dental care. Mine are fake. Bristol is happy to declare that she's all original parts.

"Sorry," I say. Too far in my head after too long in immersion.

"Are you hungry?" Dolly asks. She doesn't say 'yet', but it's in her voice.

"Kind of. I had a smoothie." But she's handing me a paper plate of the peanut chicken, rice, and greens.

There's a little bit of a flinch, just around his eyes, when Dolly calls him Nicky, but I don't know what to do with that. Bristol would.

1928. That's when Red Stripe was first made.

I eat about a quarter of the food on my plate before I stop and take stock. So far so good, but I'm done.

"So did you get ahold of your people?" Dolly's asking, leaned forward with her elbows on her knees, already finished with her second plate, drinking her second beer.

"I did," Nicolai says. He sits back very straight, holds his disposable bamboo knife and fork the European way, like Bristol.

"Which did we get, Texas or Detroit?"

Nicolai clears his throat and sets down his plate. Crosses his knife and fork on top of it with precise movements. Wipes his mouth with a paper napkin. "Neither."

"Neither," Dolly repeats.

"Not for money, drugs, guns, none of it," Nicolai says.

"Buncha pussies," Dolly says, leaning back in her chair and lighting a cigarette. "Guess it's you and me after all, Bits. And you, Nicky, if you're in. I'll pay you for your time and whatever ordinance you can give us, anyway."

"Ladies, I will help how I can. But an outright assault, we just can't do that," Nicolai says.

"What about Marquis?" I ask.

"What about them?"

"Well they've known Bristol..." I trail off.

"Last I knew, Marquis was very politely no longer returning Bristol's calls," Dolly says.

"I guess I can't blame them." Money isn't everything, after all. "Don't you have people?"

"Already contacted some of them when I was lookin' for Bristol to begin with, and tracking you down. Retired is one of them popular words," Dolly drawls, in that particular way she has when lividly angry and doing things more slowly, so as not to self-immolate. I haven't seen her like that very often. Titanium white.

Chapter Eight

"Okay, so how are we gonna do this?" Dolly asked. "Assuming it's just the three of us."

"We identify Bristol's vehicle, I compromise it, and we get her out. They don't want attention, it looks like they'll be using cars, not armored transports." How many cars, I don't know yet. And if they're networked together I can exploit that and probably get all of them at once.

"You make it sound so easy." Nicolai sifts through the stuff on the table for the bottle opener, pops the cap of his next bottle of Red Stripe.

I shrug. "It's not a real plan, is why. It's a hypothetical."

"But you are confident you can just, what did you call it, compromise a vehicle?"

"Oh yeah, that's no sweat for Bitsy," Dolly says. "Sometimes she does it for fun, just for practice."

Nicolai looks at me. "You do?"

"I do." His new regard makes me uncomfortable. Even now, a lot of people are still pretty unsure what hacking can do, and I'm not really in any hurry to quantify that for them.

"Can you show me?" he asks.

"I guess." I glance at Dolly, who drags on her cigarette and shrugs.

"What's the harm?"

"Nothing, I guess." I pull out my headset.

"Does my car need to be on?" Nicolai asks, rummaging for his keys. "Because I can—"

"Modern cars are never entirely off," I say distractedly as my headset boots up. I have a pretty good catalog of the most popular vehicles on the road and what can be compromised, on the spectrum of benign to malicious. It varies further based on conditions. Sometimes it's as simple as using salt to fool the autodriver; we did that on an eighteen wheeler once.

Nicolai's car is a forward-slung electric six speed that a company nostalgic about the Ford Mustang started putting out in the last decade. Nicolai's car is, ostensibly, fairly secure. Earlier, I noticed the little programmed icon of a lock; built in antivirus and antimalware, both good stuff. I virtually reach out into the parking lot and tap my electric fingers on the car. Nicolai has satellite radio subscriptions, GPS, autodriving that he hardly uses. Interesting. How does autodriving work with the manual transmission? It has to be both, then, so probably six speed clutchless shifting.

I magnify the floating line of code I need. I can see it through the virtual window, tinted just a micrometer darker than is probably legal. I fiddle with that code, twist it back on itself like an old fashioned wire coat hanger, and the doors unlock.

"Go sit in the car, Dolly," I say. I can hear myself, of course. Hear them in the room. The visor isn't full immersion, but interacting with the real world while working in VR is like working on dual monitors, with one of them behind you and uses tank commands instead of the elegant code.

"It's locked," Nicolai says. Dolly only scoff-laughs, and I hear the scrape of the chair, the clomp of boots as she goes outside. A few moments later, a dismayed sound comes from Nicolai. I'm not sure why he seems so sad, actually. If we're going to do this thing, I need to be a competent hacker. Maybe he just hadn't considered his stock antivirus antimalware could actually be bypassed.

"Good enough, Bitsy. come on back to us," Dolly says, back in the room next to me again.

I don't really want to do it, but I close my eyes, pull off the headset. No exit protocol necessary. "That easy," Nicolai says, shaking his head.

"Bitsy's just that good," Dolly says in what's meant to be a consoling tone. "Not just anybody's gonna be able to hack the Nickymobile, don't you worry."

"Until a moment ago, I was more worried about it being named the Nickymobile. Now, I am less sure."

"Dolly's mostly right," I say. "Not just anybody with a headset and a smartphone is going to be able to hack your car."

"But you took hardly any time."

"Also true." Practice makes perfect.

"And it's off. Or the ignition is off."

"Correct." I'm tired, and getting a headache. Really, this should be funny. It's like I performed a magic trick for him. I wouldn't even need to put the headset back on to just turn the thing on right now, with my phone, or with my contacts and implant. I could honk the horn or flash the lights, but I resist the impulse.

"I toldja she was good." I'm so glad that she isn't celebrating more loudly.

"So that's a good baseline?" I ask.

"I would say so, yes," Nicolai says, a combination of gloomy and relieved.

"I'm going to lie down now, then."

"You okay? Do you need anything?" Glimmers of nurse-maid Dolly again. It's just so *weird*.

"Just tired and a headache. Right now, I'm going to drink some water. I don't think I drank enough water today. And I'm going to go to sleep." I'm just not the kind of person that tylenol or aspirin works for.

"Should I..." Nicolai was already starting to get up.

"Don't bother, I sleep like a rock,"

"More like a hibernating bear," Dolly says. "Rocks don't make the noise you do."

"Maybe they do, just really slowly. Geologic age snoring." I go into the bathroom, close the door, and drink three cups of water. I stare at myself in the bathroom mirror while my stomach gurgles and I wonder if I'm going to lose what had actually been a pretty nice dinner. My first solid food other than candy in however long. But other than a slow roll, some flip flopping like a fish right when it feels the hook, my stomach holds steady. Good. I brush my teeth with the teeny tiny toothpaste and toothbrush provided. Nicolai and Dolly are pretty quiet when I come out. Maybe Dolly filled him in. Maybe not.

"I mean it," I say. "Keep planning. You know what I can do, Dolly."

"We will, don't you worry," Dolly says. "Just get your rest."

"No doubt," I say. My head hits the pillow, and I think of VR and the night sky and the line between sleeping and waking blurs away into stars.

Chapter Nine

I wake up and don't know where I am. Silvery moonlight comes through the thrown-open motel room curtains. Dolly sleeps sprawled on her stomach in her usual way, like a cast aside toy, and has one arm flung over Nicolai, who sleeps stiffly on his back like a vampire expecting to rise from the grave. Then I remember.

Bristol. Leaving Mexico. Nobody to help us. Red Stripe. The room feels very close, as though all the exhaled breaths of everybody who has ever slept here are still trapped.

I get up and go out into the parking lot barefoot, leaving the door ajar. I can hear the sign buzzing at the side of the road, can see the puddle of yellow light from the main office spilling onto the crushed oyster shells. Hardly any cars are here. It really could just be a murder motel and we'd never know, unless we get murdered too. I slept in my AR contacts and my eyes are dry; I feel every millimeter of every blink.

I pace up the sidewalk to the hallway of vending machines, bounce away from their constant whining hum before it catches me, white on white noise static that I'll never escape, it'll shake my skull apart. I walk almost to the office, back to the room again. I think about the real metal key that Dolly has for our room and wonder if they have a computer in there, or just a big ledger book that people sign when they arrive. An old fashioned no-tell motel, in this day and age. I stand looking at Nicolai's car, next to Dolly's Jeep. He must have locked it again after I went to sleep.

"What's up?" Dolly's behind me

"I woke up and couldn't stay in there anymore."

"Want a ginger ale?"

"What?" I turn to look at her. She's looking at me with something like compassion.

"A ginger ale. To calm down." Dolly gestures towards the vending machines with the cigarette she's about to light.

"Are you making fun of me?"

"Nah. I just didn't know if it was your stomach or what. And if it was an or what, we got stuff to add to the ginger ale."

"If you think I'm going to drink tequila and ginger ale..."

Dolly puts her hands up, leaving the cigarette on her bottom lip. "Hey, I don't judge."

"I know." I take a deep breath, count to five, let it out. If Dolly of all people thinks I need to calm down, I need to calm down.

Dolly leans against the wall by the room door and blows a smoke ring. It drifts ghost like across the parking lot towards the highway, towards the ocean, and I lose track of it. Breathe. I guess I've been sweating because it's cooling on my skin now, in the breeze, the headache in my left temple barking like a bored dog. Oh how am I going to do this? How are we going to do this?

"Tell me something about the job that went bad."

She shifts her weight, surprised, and her eyes catch the light from the motel sign. What's the expression on her face? Guilt? She's probably just tired. "Are you sure that's a good idea?"

"Just a random fact in the middle. Give me a stepping stone."

She's quiet, paper on the end of her cigarette crackling, exhaling sighs of smoke. "Yeah, I get you. Gimme a sec." I wait, counting my breaths, which don't feel so restricted anymore. "I picked the job, I guess I should say that."

Guilt, then. Weird. "We always trade around." Dolly acting like anything less than confident is almost scarier than not being able to remember what happened. Not being able to hear and retain what happened.

"Okay, yeah. Bristol wasn't in Morocco anymore because the more she traveled, the more of an electronic trail she was leaving to confuse pursuit. And before you say that you can help with that, she just wanted to globetrot and have her little adventures and overwrite their data. She was only gonna ask you as last resort."

I wait, don't feel any worse. Don't feel any better, either. Of course there was going to be pursuit. We all signed very nice amnesty contracts and then made off with both the money the contracts promised us and the diamonds that *we* had promised them. "Okay, makes sense. That isn't it, though."

"No. Just testing the waters." She takes a final drag, flicks the butt into the parking lot and there's a tiny spray of embers when it lands. "We were visiting sites. Looking for a place I'd been. Um. Trained, I guess. And—"

"You needed a file," I say, almost remembering but not really, and a sudden wave of dizziness hits me, just as hard as if I was standing on the beach and a real wave broke. Dolly catches me when my knees buckle, and I grab her arm with both hands, trying to steady myself.

"You're all gooseflesh now. Come on, back to bed. Don't go wandering in the night, okay?"

"Okay." The idea of walking back into the room doesn't stuff the breath down in my throat anymore. "We're leaving in the morning, right?"

"Right," Dolly says, but her tone says we won't if she thinks I can't.

We crawl back into our beds and I don't think I'll be able to sleep. I watch the color of light change, listen to Dolly's breathing slip into sleep breathing, listen to Nicolai's not-quite-snores. But I do drift off because the next time I open my eyes, Dolly's standing in the doorway smoking and humming to herself, while watching Nicolai do something with his car out front. "He's still spooked about your digital wizardry," she says without turning. I don't know how she knows I'm awake.

"A lot of people get that way. He has to have seen it before, right?"

"Right? You wouldn't think a guy like Nicky'd have his head in the sand, but here you go. He might talk to you about hacker-proofin' his ride."

"There are some things I can do for him."

"That's good. Lie, if you gotta. Otherwise he's gonna whine halfway across the country and back about how somebody's gonna hack his car and drive him into something, or something."

"Well. They could."

"Yeah, but why bother?"

Nicolai comes back in, also smoking. And people think my VR habit is bad. "You slept well?" he asks.

"I had my moments. You?"

"We'll be better prepared the next time we find lodgings," he says carefully. "There will be enough rooms, or enough beds, for each of us."

"Sorry to offend your sensibilities," Dolly says. There's only so many stops we can afford to make, timewise. She stands and surveys the room for anything we might've left. "Are we ready to roll?"

"How long is it from here to Kansas?" Nicolai asks. "And which car goes first?"

"Nicky, buddy, you really asking me that?"

"Sorry, Dolly. Of course you'll go first. But how long?"

"How many miles to Babylon?" I mutter, and Dolly gives me a sidelong glance.

"What now?"

"It's an old poem. Nursery rhyme. Whatever. How many miles to Babylon, three score miles and ten, can we get there by candlelight, yes and back again."

"Yeah, but does anybody ever remember what a fucking score is?" Dolly asks as we get into the Jeep.

"No, I have to look it up every time," I laugh.

"Dolly..." Nicolai says carefully.

"Christ, Nicolai, it's like, twelve hours or twenty or something, I don't fucking know. We'll drive until we get tired and get a motel again. Calm your tits. Driving across the United States takes far less effort than driving across Russia anyway, and we don't have to worry about the KGB."

"The KGB isn't—"

"Well whatever the fuck took its place, meet the new boss, same as the old boss. Bits will set up communications between our cars, won't you Bits? You got those little satellite walkie things you can program on a private network?"

I don't know why I haven't thought about earbuds before now. Or anything. "Oh...yeah. Give me a sec." I rummage in my bag for the walkies, then pull out the VR headset again. I don't need it for this, strictly speaking, but I like using it. It'll make it faster. I set up the connection, each unit absolutely only talking to the other, encrypted. I hesitate a moment over the password, and make it 3scoreMiles&10. Nobody'll have to enter a password ever, but being prepared for eventualities is always part of the game. We'll network earbuds eventually, but I guess waiting is just another natural step on taking things easy. I should get eye drops from a vending machine. Or maybe I should just not sleep in my contacts. There's an eye implant now too, I just read about it.

"Here, stick it on your windshield. Don't make that face, the adhesive won't last once the unit is removed. Flip that button to make it voice activated, then you won't have to worry about settings, just talk when you want to talk, and it'll broadcast when we talk."

"And here is where I find out that Miss Bits can be bossy as well," Nicolai says, taking the card-sized walkie.

"That's us, a pair of bossy bitches," Dolly says, grinning. "Didn't know she had it in her, didja?"

"I did not."

"Well, let's get this show on the road," Dolly says as I slap the walkie on our dashboard. Though I guess it's a drivie, in this context. I run our route into the GPS and Dolly looks it over, makes a noise of disappointment. "I was kinda looking forward to getting my kicks on Route 66."

"Well, we'll have to get somebody arrested in a more convenient location, then. Or break into Area 51."

"Is Area 51 real?" Nicolai asks. These cheap little walkies still have pretty good audio, I'm always surprised.

"Like, do they have aliens and the remains of a crashed spacecraft there real, or is it a real government site real?" Dolly wants him to ask about aliens, she really does.

"I take from your tone that I don't really have a right answer," he says mournfully.

"Aw, don't feel too bad, Nicky."

"Thank you, Dolly. Thank you for being such a stalwart friend." She laughs so hard, I think I'm going to have to reach over and take the wheel to keep us from crashing and dying before we even leave California, but Dolly keeps it on the road. She always keeps it on the road.

"No problem. Now we'll try to push 'til eleven anyway, then get brunch like the fancy assholes we are, and maybe Bits can do a status check on the projected convoy."

Chapter Ten

We have our brunch closer to lunch, in the kind of no name place that Dolly has an affinity for seeking out. The menus are augmented with holographs, spinning pictures of each dish with the ingredients list and allergy warnings, and I spend probably too long fiddling with that just for the pleasure of it, after the waitress brings waters and a coffee pot.

"Bits, gotta pick something," Dolly says after awhile, and I get the sense that the waitress has probably circled back around a few times and been waved away.

"Sorry." I pick French toast with a side of bacon, because eggs are horrific to me right now. Dolly orders a full on lumberjack spread, bacon, eggs, sausage, toast, all of it. Nicolai orders eggs Benedict, but even as the waitress leaves to put in the order, he mutters that he's probably going to be unhappy with it and should've picked something else.

"Well, now's the time," Dolly says.

"No, no, I might just be pleasantly surprised," he says. "I don't like making trouble for the kitchen."

"Alrighty," Dolly says, but she rolls her eyes and I stifle a laugh. There aren't a whole lot of other people here, though more filter in as we wait for our food. Lots of truckers, and lots of family vacationers, by the looks of it.

I wonder where the closest actual town is, and if locals ever come here to eat, or if they just come here to work. We're just off the highway somewhere in the middle of Arizona, where rock chimneys jut up out of the desert hardpan, and the mountains purple the hazy, distant horizon. The waitress sets the plate down in front of me and I jump. "Sorry, honey," she says, squinting at me.

"It's my fault, I wasn't paying attention."

"Gonna only get more jittery, you keep downing coffee like that," Dolly says, already shoveling food in her mouth. "Plus we'll have to make a bajillion rest stops."

"This is my last cup," I say. How many did I drink already? One at the motel. Two here. Three? Coffee doesn't make me jittery, why would Dolly say that?

I poke at my French toast; nicely browned, dusted with powdered sugar. The syrup decanter on the table is unlabeled, but there's a 97% chance that it's flavored corn syrup and has nothing to do with maple. Maple syrup costs more per gallon than gasoline, maybe we should hijack a maple syrup truck when this is all done. Is that classy enough for Bristol?

I look over at Dolly, mentally play the "where's Dolly's gun?" game. She isn't in full riot gear right now, so in a tank top and jeans, it's hard to hide one. Maybe an ankle holster? She definitely has a knife, anyway. I've lost track of which states are open carry; we might be allowed to go strapped all the time and just aren't. None of the truckers are carrying.

I watch Nicolai fork into the poached egg on his plate. The yolk oozes out across the Canadian bacon and English muffin, mixed with the sunny Hollandaise, and a surprised smile crossed his face. "I'm happy that I was wrong," he says after the first bite.

"Well that's good," Dolly says, half done already. I start eating. There's no way I can finish this, but Dolly probably can. The French toast doesn't taste like anything, not even after I douse in it syrup, but it isn't the French toast's fault. I'm starting to get afterimages of things around the diner, particularly if they're shiny, or silhouetted against light, like Dolly, who sits facing the door but with her back against the white curtained window. And the AR contacts don't help.

"I'll be right back," I say, and stand up unsteadily. Dolly says...something...but I can't really hear her as I make my way to the bathroom, jaw clenched, breathing through my nose. It's single occupant, the door hanging open, and it's through sheer willpower that I close the door firmly but quietly, lock it, and then lean my forearms on my knees and throw up the French toast and all that coffee and then continue heaving until tears are streaming down my face but nothing else will come up. At least my hair is short and I don't have to worry about that too.

My vision statics out when I flush and then stand upright, and I hope I don't just pass out on the floor right here. I wash my face with the flat fake floral hand soap and dry off with the scratchy brown paper towels. There's a certain smell those brown paper towels always have when they're wet. I rinse my mouth and dig into my pockets, hoping for a tin of mints, a piece of gum, something. Nope. It's okay, they sell stuff like that at the register. It feels like my eyes are minutely shifting from side to side, but I can't see in the mirror to see if that's real. The static still hangs in my vision, and past experience tells me what kind of headache is breaking over me like a wave.

A knock at the door. Kind of brusque, maybe it isn't their first knock.

I clear my throat. "Just a minute," I call. I pull the door open right as a woman, holding a little girl's hand raises her fist to knock again. We look at each other for a long moment, and I feel like maybe the woman expects me to apologize, but I can't find the words, or the right facial expression, and eventually the little girl just shoves past me and the woman follows.

Dolly meets me partway across the room. "You okay?"

No. "Time will tell," I say. I want to crawl under a table and put a blanket over my head and shake until I pass out.

"Nicolai paid, so we're ready to leave if you are."

"Thank you, Nicolai. I just want to get some mints."

"If you say so," Dolly says, hovering.

"And then I'll hop into VR, get some more intel while we're on the move, like we said. Make it that much harder to track me." She eyes me dubiously, but relents and goes outside.

They do have mints. And painkillers, but not any kind that'll help me, so I just chew three mints before I jam the rest of them in my pocket and go outside. The parking lot is so very bright, and I close my eyes and fumble with my sunglasses, dropping them twice before just giving up.

"Bits, are you sure you're—" Dolly starts.

What does she want me to say? We don't have the luxury of me sitting this out. "You keep asking me that. We need to know what's happening to Bristol and neither of you knows how to do this." Eyes squinted almost closed, I get out my VR headset and lean my head back on the seat. Dolly's still talking, maybe to me, maybe to Nicolai, but I'm already focused on the virtual, looking for the coordinates of the Kansas location from the files I copied. I can play back what she said later, see if it was important.

Things are very flat in Kansas, and the sky seems very big. There's a lot of buildings, old and new mixed together, and the street in places is brick. Train tracks, the old kind, not for a monorail or hyperloop. The building I need is concrete, of course, that institutional block that's been so cheap and popular for so long. The fence around it doesn't have razorwire the way the Texas facility does, but I have the overwhelming feeling that security here is a lot tighter. I take a couple blinks to make sure my avatar is appropriately nondescript Army, with appropriate at-a-glance credentials. This facility is far more subtle with its visible security levels, no patrolling people or programs visible. I pass through the gates unchecked, approach the front door.

It's keycard locked, but I know how to bypass those in person, and VR is life's digital mirror. I want to avoid tripping every alarm, avoid causing the slightest suspicion. I'm on high alert for any communications, changes, anything to do with me cracking this and entering the domain. The last thing we need is for me to screw this up, to screw anything up.

This would be easier in full immersion, without my real life ears receiving data, without my head throbbing against the gently rocking car seat, the sun hot on my hair, tasting mint and I-just-threw-up. But I take my time and double check my work at every step. Then I'm in, cautiously continuing through the server halls, admiring the coding, dipping into data here and there. I copy the list of vehicles in the motor pool, and the list of what's requisitioned for near future transfers. I send that to Dolly's phone to keep her busy. She doesn't typically mess with me when I've got the headset on, but she's worried and worry makes people make mistakes.

Next I locate the holding cells. They probably neutralize the language. Kind of like when they say "enhanced interrogation"; pretty much everybody knows that means a particular range of unpleasant things.

Fuck, my head hurts. My left temple feels like it used to be an egg, but that egg broke and the yolk and albumen are running down the side of my face in liquid pain. There's a throb to it, a long and steady throb, and I try to concentrate on my breathing while taking the programmed stairs down to the programmed basement.

It's a waste to have personnel hanging out trying to watch for little changes in code. It's improbable anybody will notice what I'm doing. I can't say I've never been caught, but I can count the times on one hand. At least one of the times was a deliberate; I was working with another hacker and diverted attention off the higher value target and onto me instead.

There are more people in holding than just Bristol, and my digital ghost passes three occupied areas before reaching her. She's got a TV, and even a remote, but the remote is locked to five channels, without power and without volume control. It's tuned very slightly too loud. She doesn't have earbuds in, or contacts, or I'd be able to send her a message. No camera into the cell, or I'd be able to see her. I'm scared to see her.

Her file is on the door and I make a copy while I scan through it quick. Height, weight, still no good ID. Transfer date is pushed to three days from now, instead of tomorrow like the original files. Recovery time, before the exchange is made. I feel a deep terrible chill. Mostly they've just done environmental manipulation, too hot or too cold, the TV thing, not letting her sleep. Mostly basics, mostly physically harmless, and I can envision Bristol doing social backflips to get these people to see her as human, to have empathy, to take pity on her and make that connection that would stop them from hurting her. But yeah, they still hurt her anyway.

There's a side note about her teeth being all intact. I wonder if I'm going to throw up again.

A frustrated note from one of her handlers, because they have her on a light level of sedation that will normally lower a person's inhibitions, make them inclined to be talkative. Not so with Bristol. Or rather, she's talkative but on zero of the topics they have an interest in. I imagine her discussing this year's Paris fashion show in excruciating, exquisite detail. I can hack Bristol's door, but there isn't anywhere for her to get to. We aren't in Kansas right now, and there are a lot of armed personnel in that building. Bristol is relentlessly hopeful; or at least I have to assume she still is. That she looks upon this as a temporary inconvenience, another experience to write about in her little locked leather-bound diary, memoirs that she says she'll publish when she's old and it won't matter anymore.

I make myself read the details again. They hurt her, but not enough that she needs medical attention. She'll be operational, when we stop the convoy. They've got a note about her belongings and I scan that. No diary, that's good. It looks like she had her purse, her coat, her phone and earbuds. Purse full of makeup and actual paper ticket stubs and fashion magazines, folding flats, an anti-digital surveillance scarf, and a dress from a capsule vending machine. Bus station locker key. My breathing feels funny and I do a scan to make sure I'm not compromised, our location a beacon for law enforcement in a fifty mile radius. But no, my equipment is secure. I'm still 'standing' in the hallway outside Bristol's holding cell. When the files are done copying I walk away. How many people are here anyway? How many people can they hold? It seems like a lot. Domestic terrorism is such an easily manipulated idea.

There's another exit here and I check it over carefully to make sure it's a real thing and not an 'alarms will sound if opened' trick door.

It's so bright in VR outside that I recoil and have nowhere to go, my head already against the Jeep headrest. I pull the headset off, squeeze my eyes shut again almost immediately. My ears pop-squeal into white noise, and there's a hand on my arm, something on my face. Something wet on my face. Am I crying? Poor Bristol.

I bring my hand up and it's swatted away, and Dolly's voice pushes through my hearing fuckup, clear as day. "You got a gusher, see if you can hold this here. If you can't, keep out of my way." I hold a cloth against my face. A bandanna, probably. Or one of those digital scarves. It bothers me that I didn't run into any cybersecurity measures. Are they just that much better than me? Am I just that much better than them? I can't make either option make sense.

Dolly must've gone away for a little while, or maybe she sent Nicolai away, because then she's nudging something cold against the back of my other hand, and I crack my eyes open enough to see a to-go cup, a straw. I fumbled at it, and Dolly just sticks the straw in my mouth. It's sugared-up iced coffee and I must've told Dolly about how sugar makes things bearable, about how coffee or hard drugs are the only things that touch these headaches for me.

"You okay?" Dolly asks, when I sit up a little straighter, take the cloth away to squint at it. That's blood all right. I sniff and scrub at my nose, looking around but I can't remember for what. Oh, my sunglasses, on the dashboard. With them on, I'm almost able to bear the world. "Do you want to ride with Nicolai? His car has, y'know, a roof. Windows, tinted."

"I don't really know," I say. "No."

"About which?"

"Either." I drink some more coffee, first happy to have it and then sure it's the biggest mistake ever as my stomach curls on itself. I turn my head away from the straw. The ice rattles as Dolly jams it into a cup holder. We aren't in the diner parking lot anymore. "Where...?"

"We relocated to that truck stop right off the highway, to gas up and get road snacks and other incidentals. Plus, I had a feeling this would be good for you. Nicolai is very good at following instructions, luckily, so I didn't have to leave him babysitting you. He doesn't seem to be very comfortable with the sight of blood."

"I'm standing right here," Nicolai says from outside my field of vision.

"Yeah, not like I forgot," Dolly says. "I'm just fillin' Bits in. She missed you goin' a whiter shade of pale."

"You have to understand the further implications I read into the sudden fountain of blood coming out of our friend's face, I was concerned for her. I don't faint at the sight of blood. I would be a terrible businessman in this particular venue if that were the case."

"Yeah, you would," Dolly agrees.

"We're wasting time," I say.

"What's our deadline then?" Dolly asks, banter gone. I wonder a lot just how thin that banter veneer is, how much of the joke and swagger is part of the put-on dangerous woman image that lets her interact with normal people. Dolly is definitely the most genuinely dangerous of us three. Me and Bristol can both handle ourselves in our own ways, but Dolly gets this extra sparkle when things are particularly thrilling.

"Well, we've got more time than tomorrow. Transport is in three days. But none of the records say where she's going, just that she's being moved." I close my eyes again. If I can just focus on this for a little while, run the logistics, it'll at least keep the pain at arm's length. Maybe. At least I can still think.

"But she's okay, you think," Dolly says.

"I think she'll *be* okay. Bristol is resilient."

"You mean she's still gonna be pretty." She's joking but not-joking. Bristol's cultivation of appearance, of expectations built on her beauty, is something that she's worked on like somebody who sharpens knives for a living. It's all on purpose, it's all calculated.

"Also that."

Chapter Eleven

Back on the road, Dolly mutes our end of the conversation on the walkies. "You mentioned enhanced interrogation," Dolly says.

Did I? "I did." I can see no upside to talking about this. I can't bring myself to look at the files again right now, to see what exactly that meant for Bristol. My head feels like one of those plastic 3D puzzles with the big chunky pieces, and like the pieces aren't fit together right.

"Look, I'm not going to get all MKULTRA on you, because fun as that is to drop into conversations, it's got nothing to do with that. But somebody somewhere along the way figured ways of partitioning the brain using hypnosis, right? Even from yourself?"

"Oh. Yeah, right. I know that." Some people call it brainhacking, which I don't think is the right terminology to use exactly, but nobody asked me.

"Well. It's something I've got." I think I'm not really surprised. She's looking at me expectantly, like she's never told anybody—but no, that's not it. She's waiting for me to static out and reboot again. "Like, I know how to do it. And there's. Other stuff. That I can't access myself."

"But what's that got to do with Bristol?" I should've asked something else but I can't.

"She knows about mine."

Oh, great. That's the best. "A smart enough interrogator can feel along those barriers."

"Also true. But it takes a long, long, long time. Kind of like...a dictionary hack?"

"I get you." It can. It depends on your setup. I imagine Dolly and Bristol holed up in a hotel somewhere, Bristol doing her nails and Dolly breaking her guns down like praying the rosary, practicing their autohypnosis. But I was there too. I clearly have something walled off too, but the way I react when I get close to it isn't how I think these things normally work. The more I think about it the more the throb in my head looms again, the more my thoughts are scribbled out with a black marker.

"So how much..." she trails off, takes a breath. "I guess if her files said she talked, you would've said something."

"Oh, Bristol has talked a lot. About all kinds of inane and inconsequential things. Her interrogator put a note in the file complaining about it."

Dolly laughs, loud and surprised, and I'm in too much pain to even flinch anymore. "That's just perfect, isn't it? We shouldn't expect anything less."

"We shouldn't." I can't keep my eyes closed because it makes me feel worse, but I also can't look at her. I try to fix my gaze on a distant point on the horizon. Isn't that what you're supposed to do if you're seasick? There are things Dolly can't access; that means somebody has passwords, there are passwords, passcodes, passphrases, and this is where I lose the string again and either nod off or pass out.

I dream about concrete walls with bright green moss growing in the cracks. I dream about a squarely spiraling hedge maze that has a pit in the middle. I don't know what's in the pit, but it's loud and it's angry. I'm afraid, but not of what's in the pit. What's in the pit is mine, and I have no reason to be afraid of it, but as I try to get to it, I keep tripping on my untied shoelaces. Bristol is whispering in my ears, telling me about the beaches in Morocco, the seashells that you can find there, little pink ones like fingernails and big white clamshells and sometimes, if you're lucky, you can still find the spiraling chambered fossils of ammonites. I put an ammonite to my ear but I don't hear the ocean I hear static, overwhelming static, and one of the walls of the maze just falls apart. Then I hear Dolly, talking about how sure, getting replacement muscles hurt, but it hurt less than having to replace an entire arm, and it was lucky we made so much money on our jobs, because that meant her arm was like a real one. Bleeding edge cybernetics, so real that they bleed, she says, laughing and holding out her bleeding, torn-up arm, glittering with shrapnel that's seashells.

When I wake up, it's 5:30 am, my AR contacts dryly glued to my eyeballs but still reading, in an unfamiliar room. Dolly and Nicolai are talking somewhere, bickering. I push myself upright, and the room wavers, spins, resolves. Does Dolly have a fake arm and I forgot? What happened to her original arm? Does Dolly have fake muscles and that's why she's so strong?

"Morning sunshine," Dolly says. A covered tray is on one of the tables; room service I guess, but the coffee maker is part of the wall, steaming and ready to be poured.

"Morning," I say. "Did you sleep at all?"

"I did. How'd you sleep?"

"Okay." I'm looking-not-looking at her arms, bared in a tank top. They look like they match but that's part of it, right?

Having enough money so everything looks the way it should. She does have a scar on her left shoulder I don't remember, thin and pale and curving back down through her shirt. I'm surprised I didn't notice it when we were spraying each other with sunscreen on our drive up from Mexico. No I'm not. Dolly has a lot of scars.

"Here, sit down, have some coffee. I didn't order you any food, but they've got a blender if you want a slushy."

"I don't want anything," I say, and she eyes me skeptically, then dumps coffee in the blender with ice and sugar.

"Bits, should you check on our timeline?" Nicolai asks.

"Give her a fucking minute," Dolly growls over the blender.

"I'll do it," I say, because I'm supposed to. And it isn't like I need much encouragement to get out the headset, not with the building tension of whatever it is we'll have to do in order to get Bristol out of trouble, not with how I constantly feel in the real world right now. "It'll be fine," I say, reassuring Dolly or myself.

"Mmmhmm," Dolly says, in very much a 'you're a grownup who can make your own decisions even when they're terribly wrong' kind of way.

I've already got the headset powered up, though, and am slipping it over my eyes. I'm in Texas again. No, Kansas. I walk through the gates again, the front door again. I can see other code activity this time, and I'm careful to behave within expected parameters, get past where there's now a guard, automated or staffed, just inside. My coded clearance disguise is good enough to not trigger any alarms that I notice. Every time I do this, I get a better sense of their limitations and protocols.

Security is only as good as the space between the chair and the keyboard, as the saying goes.

The motor pool is actually staffed with security. It's the Uncanny Valley game again; I can't say what exactly makes me realize the patrols aren't automated, but I know for certain that they are staffed. The records are automated, though, and I grab a capture of the next seven calendar days. In fact, just to make sure, I go a few weeks back and grab that data too. Maybe it'll line up with Bristol's original arrest, I don't know. I don't remember, from the files, and Dolly's been doing a lot of things, but synchronizing our watches isn't one of them.

"Is everything in expected order, ma'am?" a voice at my elbow asks.

"Yes, it seems to be," I say, glancing at the personnel member. That's the thing about military avatars, they always display their rank. "Thanks for checking in on me, Lieutenant. Sometimes I get lost in all these records. We understand the need for redundancy, of course, but..." I trail off with a wry smile.

"Of course, ma'am. It can be overwhelming." The Lieutenant salutes and continues on, only to stop again when another officer enters the motor pool area.

I noodle around with some more records, then notice the motor pool's connection with the rest of the server at large. Military grade indeed. Nobody just casually standing next to my avatar can see what I'm looking at, but if one of those security personnel decide I'm acting suspiciously, or if somebody deeper in the data structure does, all sorts of alarms will go off. If I just put a little line of code here, and here, then I'll get pinged when the convoy leaves.

It isn't like anything can actually hurt me in VR. There's the possibility of backtracing and drone strikes, that happens and nobody's a fan. But the problem with making the virtual as real as possible is your mind sometimes makes your body think that things are happening. And there's the hypnosis thing. Oh shit the hypnosis thing.

"Not trying for a vehicle above your pay grade, are you Captain?" The other officer, major, hasn't really neared, but near and far are relative concepts in VR.

"No sir, double checking a vehicle I already turned in."

"Good diligence," the major says, and right when I think it's the end of it, he continues, "I don't want to hear about mileage discrepancies because somebody's running a side project out of here."

"Sir?" No system alarms have begun, but my fight or flight is ramping up, shaking my concentration. This conversation is no good.

"Like this operation," the major says. "Do you know anything about this operation?" The major gestures at the files I just copied, the two vehicle prisoner convoy. "Almost too small to be a real thing stateside. We don't use only two vehicles for anything."

"I can't say I'm familiar, sir. It isn't my project."

A security officer passes us once, twice, and then is joined by another just as I'm stepping away. I should've stepped away sooner. An alarm goes off, and I flinch, but it isn't for me. The major's uniform pixelates. Tracers are going back through his connections, all that streaming code, automated systems faster than human thought.

"Excuse me, ma'am, I'm going to have to ask you to return to finish your business another time," one member of security says to me. "This guy isn't supposed to be here. We've had a few hacker incursions lately."

"That's fine, Private, thank you for your time. I think I've gotten everything straightened out." I leave the motor pool, hesitate. Should I try to help the other hacker? Why are they asking about Bristol's convoy too? I ping what I can remember of his connection, a tiny little ghost ping following Homeland's backtrace. Also in Kansas. I really wish I had a good way to get information out of Dolly, or information out of Dolly that I can stand to hear without my brain turning into soup.

I pull the headset off and Dolly's already handing me another bandanna. "Thanks."

"What's up?"

"Convoy is going to be two vehicles. I grabbed some personnel files but didn't look at them yet. Somebody else was hacking the same info at the same time I was, and got caught."

"What does caught even mean in this context?"

"Not a whole lot if you're me. That guy, they know where he is, which means I know where he is. I'm not sure if they're just going to scoop him up or strike him or what."

"Well, where is he? Anyplace useful? We're low on helpful bodies here. Might be somebody we can bring aboard."

"Maybe. I feel bad seeing that and just walking away, anyway."

"Nicolai, you're awful quiet. Don't have anybody else workin' this on the side, do you?"

"I do not," he says.

"Well," Dolly says, shoving the coffee icee she just made at me, with that particular grin. "I guess we might as well warm up by drag racing Homeland."

Chapter Twelve

Dolly breaks 110 as we cross the Kansas state line, the wind around the topless jeep tunneling past the upright windshield with an unbelievable roar. Maybe in a panic, maybe sensibly, I fight the impulse to just crouch in my foot well and wait for us to either reach our destination or for it to be all over when a deer decides to step onto the highway at the wrong second. Nicolai initially complained about the sudden change in plans, the mad dash from the hotel, but Dolly ignored him. His muscle car can beat us, no question, but he's letting Dolly take the lead.

"How far did you say, Bits?" Dolly yells. It takes a few tries, and damn it, I should've put in earbuds when I woke up.

"Cut north here and maybe thirty miles?"

"And you're sure Homeland'll be onto him too?"

"Pretty sure."

"And what's their timeline?"

"Christ, Dolly, I don't know where their nearest drone site is, or personnel. I don't know enough about how Homeland operates to—"

"What?" Dolly yells.

I pull the headset up. The nearest real base, as opposed to the weird black site where they've got Bristol, is three hundred miles away. "For a drone, hour and a half. Personnel, much longer. If they follow the speed limit."

"Ping the guy. Tell him to be ready."

"Like he's just going to run out into the parking lot and hop in the back," I yell. Everything about this is ridiculous, down to the last detail.

"He will if he knows what's good for him."

She isn't wrong. I ping the connection I had for the guy, but he's smart, he already pulled the plug. I follow the code, look for other nearby connections. He's in a motel, was using their regular wireless. I find the router; the phone line is still separate from the internet, imagine. It's digital, though. I find his room and ring the phone. One ring, two rings. If it was me, I wouldn't answer the phone. If it was me, I'd already be gone. Six rings, seven. I'm about to hang up when the line opens. "Hello?"

The VR headset doesn't have a mic but voice to text is practically human, finally. "Hello, Major. Can I assume you want evac?" I text, and the phone spits it out dutifully in a voice similar to mine. Uncanny Valley in everyday life.

"Who is this? Why are you calling me? Did you say Major? Are you seriously trolling me right now?" No audio either, of course, just scrolling text on my end.

"I'm not the one who got caught. Do you want an out or no?"

"You were also...you were the one...fine, yes. Tell me when and where."

I check the GPS. Ten minutes, unless something terrible happens. "Ten minutes, edge of the parking lot. Turn off all your equipment."

"Okay." He hangs up, and I pull the headset down around my neck, look at Dolly.

"Look, I know you wanted more personnel or whatever, but there's no guarantee this guy will work well with us. And he was sloppy." Why am I arguing? It's not like I want to just leave him.

"You just want to be the only hacker," Dolly says.

"I just don't want to get killed by an amateur." I dig around in my bag for the shrink wrapped earbuds, link mine up to my phone and the walkie, lean over and plug one into Dolly's ear. She takes the other one and settles it without swerving even a little bit.

"I agree," Nicolai is saying. "Dolly, are you sure you want to add an unknown element at this point?"

"Buddy, the convoy hasn't left yet, we got time to get him and we got time to vet him. If he seems like a clown we can cut him loose or leave him in a culvert or whatever, I don't care. But if there's a chance he's going to be a help, a real help, I wanna take that chance. So, I'm sorry for the unplanned detour, I know plans are very important to you, Nicolai. But this is what we're doing."

I sigh. She isn't wrong, we need more people. "If nothing else we can find out why he was looking into the same data as me. Seems like a coincidence is unlikely, right?"

"I'm not sure I believe in coincidences," Dolly says. "Here's the exit?" She doesn't wait for an answer, just slows to a clearly far more reasonable 55 miles an hour for the off ramp. "Where's the motel?"

"Left," I say, gripping the door handle. At least if Dolly rolls the Jeep, our deaths will be quick and merciful. At least my head doesn't hurt right now anymore.

A tall skinny guy...no, it's a girl, angular featured and in an oversized jacket, with a backpack. She's standing on the grassy expanse between the motel parking lot and the road, her head craning anxiously this way and that, towards the highway and the other way. The other way is where the drones will come from, I think. They're sure to be scrambling now, hustling in this direction between 85 and 110 miles an hour. Or more, depending on the make and model. Or less. There are laws about what drones could be used on American soil of course, but if none of this was on the up and up to begin with, those laws are kind of out the window. Like Bristol's interrogations. Her detainment, I think, is probably justified. But that isn't the point.

Dolly doesn't even really come to a complete stop, just kind of skid-slides up to the shoulder doing twenty and the girl's already running and throws her backpack into the back first, then as the Jeep fishtails and the speedometer dips below ten, gets in herself. It's a fairly adept hop, a swift folding of lanky limbs. Dolly steers into the slide, and loops back down the road to the highway onramp again. I lean back, set of earbuds in my fist, and I loop the kid into the walkie signals.

"Your equipment is powered off?"

"Yeah, I did that as soon as we hung up," she says. "Who are you people?"

"Don't matter right now. Buckle up, buttercup," Dolly says.

I glance back; I've always been a terrible judge of age, so can't tell if she's a teenager and just inexperienced, or mid-twenties like us and careless. "What's your handle?"

"Null," she says after an uncomfortable pause.

"I'm Bits, this is Dolly. The guy in the other car, when you see him, is Nicolai."

"Bits?" she asks. "Just Bits?" She's suddenly wide eyed and excited in a way totally different from terror at Dolly's driving.

"Yeah, why?" I turn back around before I get sick in her lap.

"You're the one who hangs the stars in VR," she says. "You're a fucking ghost story."

"I'm a ghost story?" I ask. It hadn't occurred to me what other hackers thought of me. Or if they thought of me at all.

"Yeah. Private node, long immersions. Nobody's been able to track you, not even close, but there's code devoted to seeing how long you're online for. And every time you go offline, there's a big rumor mill about that. Especially this last time."

"I didn't know."

"Classic Bits," Dolly says, laughing. "So what, she's a VR legend?"

"She is, yeah. I guess that makes it make more sense now, how you found me so easily. Both online and in person."

"It's not like I'm the only one in the world who could've accomplished that. Especially with the way you had your protocols set up."

"I thought my protocols..." She stops. I glance back at Null, and her cheekbones are sunburn red. "Maybe you can teach me."

"Oh God," I say. Dolly's just whooping laughter over this.

"It's like an old kung Fu movie, where the cocky hero is accidentally schooled by the master and then seeks to be educated," she says.

"Yeah, Dolly, just like that." I roll my eyes. "Yeah, I guess I can teach you."

"Wait, that's it? You're internet famous and that's all you're gonna say about it?" Dolly asks.

"What else am I supposed to say about it?"

"I dunno. Anything. Literally anything."

"I...well it's not like it's a *good* thing, to be internet famous. It's kind of better if nobody'd ever noticed me at all."

"I think that's part of why too. You just do things, you don't showboat or claim credit," Null says helpfully.

"The stars," Dolly says distantly.

"Yeah, the stars. In the VR immersion, there aren't any stars. Weren't any stars. Just the moon. It bugs me. It's not like the mainframe doesn't have the processing power for it. They just didn't want to put in the work. So I did."

"The stars," Dolly says again, shaking her head. I'm so glad she's going a more normal speed now. "Bits, you do always surprise me."

"What, you don't think the stars are important?"

"I guess I don't really think about them. And I definitely don't think much about virtual reality."

You can say that again. "Wait, Null, why were you looking at that data?"

"For the upcoming transport?" Null asks. "They're planning on going to a site that was decommissioned in the late 90's, early century, and there's a lot of tech there that people have speculated on for a long time, but nobody's been able to get in. It's offline."

"But why do you know about the transport to begin with?" Dolly looks at me, a little enough twitch that she could've been checking the mirrors, but I catch it.

"It was a total fluke, I'm into old tech and I was poking around looking for other stuff and there was a flagged association with this arrest file. And then the convoy is really weird and—"

"Old tech," I repeat, because it sounds both totally possible and also a lie and I'm rapidly reaching my saturation point. I can't see what Bristol would have to do with old tech. Unless it has to do with data from the diamonds, but she didn't talk about that at all. And doesn't really care about most of it. Just the Fabergé egg. I wonder if she just left it in Morocco like an abandoned puppy.

"Well I guess it's lucky that we found you," Dolly says, like she doesn't at all believe it, but what else are we gonna do. "Bitsy, maybe check what we're looking at?"

"Yeah, I'll do that," I say, pulling up those personnel files I skimmed. Six DHS staff, even gender split. Maybe one day I'll get my shit together about what military ranks mean, or maybe it won't really matter in my life anymore, but a female Captain, former Army, is the highest ranked person tapped for this. The personnel will be in pretty standard body armor, each have a sidearm. No weapons on the vehicles. "Hey, do you have a gun?" I probably should've been paying better attention.

"A gun? No, I don't have a gun." Null's voice cracks, and her eyes widen, and I try to decide if she's really just a teenager after all. Maybe a runaway. Well, worse people than us could've found her.

"Do you know how to use a gun?" Dolly asks.

"I've been to the range with my dad," she says after a second. "You don't think we're going to have to shoot people do you?"

"There's no 'we' shooting people, kiddo," Dolly says. "We'll give you a taser or something."

"But everybody else is going to have guns?"

"Probably. I think I've got a vest that'll fit you, or maybe Nicolai does. Nicky, you're quiet again. You know that makes me nervous."

"I just did not see where you needed my input," he says. "You seemed to have covered the bases."

"Is he Russian?" Null asks. She didn't quite seem to know how loud or quietly she could talk with the earbuds.

"Da, comrade," Nicolai says dryly.

"You got a spare vest or not, Nicky?"

"I have one that might suit, yes, I only saw our new friend briefly."

"Wait can...can somebody explain what we're doing?"

"We are hijacking that transport you found so interesting," Nicolai says.

"Oh."

We whip past a 'speed checked by aircraft' sign and I check again. Still nothing in our vector. I cast my net wider, and there are the blips, those little connections of the remote drones scrambling to Null's motel. They've still got about twenty minutes, and right as I cycle away, the first ground vehicle comes into that vector as well. I hope they just find Null's empty room and leave things alone without detaining anybody or anything. Hotel staff put up with too much shit as it is.

"Dolly, hey, what's the plan after we get Bristol?" Things are crackling on the edges of my vision again. The top of my head is just going to come right off. "Is it one of these old tech places like Null is talking about?"

"We don't need to worry about that right this second, Bitsy."

I look at Dolly, hands at ten and three, eyes on the road. "You could've just said no. That's not a no."

"You are correct."

"This site has the potential to have much lucrative merchandise there," Nicolai says.

Is that true, or is that what Dolly told him to get him on board? "I really need you to tell me the truth, here," I say.

"I have never lied to you," Dolly says, looking at me steadily for a moment. I believe her. We don't lie to each other. If only I could figure out what's wrong. I look at the scar on her shoulder and try to decide if it's old or new. "And I tried to tell you everything when we were still in Mexico, remember?"

The static, the pain, the buzz of the razor on my scalp. Tigers. "I remember." Nobody says anything for awhile, and then I get a little bell icon in my AR. It's the tracking code I left on the transport vehicles in the motor pool. "They're on the move now," I say.

"Motherfuck." Dolly makes a face, looks at a mile marker as it whips past. "Light up the route to our rendezvous. Not like we needed time to plan or anything."

Chapter Thirteen

"Nicky, you got a taser or a stun gun or something that our new friend can use?"

"You are aware of my stock, including a number of actual guns that—"

"I don't mind the taser or whatever, it's okay," Null says quickly.

I'm not sure how up for ambushing and shooting people I am, actually. I think of the gunshots going off like fireworks in my skull, even though noise isn't really a problem for me. Lights are. The wrong thoughts, apparently. I think about Bristol getting as far away from me and Dolly as she can and then getting arrested on purpose. Was Will that close on her trail? On ours? What were we *doing*?

"I got beanbags for my shotgun," Dolly says. "So we can do that if we want." She looks at me. "You got rubber bullets?"

"No," I say. "I don't know." I've never had to draw my gun during one of our jobs. Wait, that's not true. But I've never had to take the safety off.

"Nicky, how many tasers we got?"

"I only have two," he says.

"Oh, are they the ones we dueled with that time?" Dolly asks, laughing.

"They are."

"You two dueled with...you know what, never mind. It's fine." I wish, suddenly and strongly, for water. I should drink more water, hydration helps with all kinds of things. Though rest stops are rife with surveillance. Everything is.

"I want to hear it," Null says in a small voice. This poor kid's going to bail out of the back next time we slow down. Not everybody's equipped to handle Dolly. I hope she knows the right way to roll.

"It ain't exactly a common thing, taser duels," Dolly says. "At least not in my experience."

"Shocking," I say, leaning over to see if there's bottled water under my seat. I'm going to regret this when I sit back up again.

"Well, you spend enough time around enough rich Russians, and enough bottles of vodka get consumed, some wacky shit is bound to happen. And this one time, we were in a pretty nice place too, weren't we? Bristol was there. Wherever the Russian Riviera would be considered, the Adriatic Sea or Black Sea or someplace, on somebody's yacht, everybody very drunk, and I don't know how the topic came up but it turned out Nicolai had a case that had matching tasers in it. The kind that shoot out the little line that sticks into a person, and then shocks 'em. You know?"

"I know," Null says.

"So we did it old fashioned duel style, two of us back to back, and paced it off. It was a yacht, okay, but not twenty paces big, I forget what we did instead, me and Nicolai. Were you here for this, Bits?"

"Nope." I sit up, sway a little against my seatbelt with the head rush. No water. I think I'd decided to go to Tokyo or something where I could have actual fun; boats and bikinis are not within my interests.

"Anyway, we paced off and we turned, and actually pulled our triggers at the same time, but Nicky missed and I didn't." Dolly grins. "But we were already dressed for swimming, so once he was done twitching on the boat deck, we all went for a swim and everything was fine."

"Sounds like a blast," I say. It does not.

"Well, maybe we'll do it again sometime," Dolly says.

"No, no I will not," Nicolai says. "But you are welcome to use the tasers."

"You're a pal, Nicolai, thanks. So yeah, Null, that's you settled. Maybe Bits will want one, too, I dunno." She glances at me and I shrug. The pain has shifted more into pressure across my cheekbones and wrapped around my temples, like somebody lined my VR goggles with barbed wire. "It's not like DHS will shoot to wound," Dolly says. I maybe lost some time again.

I rummage in my bag, and find a couple of candy bars, no water. "Can we stop? I'm dying of thirst."

"We're kind of on a timer here Bitsy," Dolly says, her tone strained enough that even I notice.

"I know." In AR I pull up the moving dots of the transport, two cars, and our moving dot. The area where we hope to intersect; we need to get there before them. I'm tired and my head hurts and I'm so thirsty I want to cry.

"Okay we'll stop and I'll run in," Dolly says finally. "Unless anybody else needs anything?" Nobody takes her up on it. Dolly's off the next exit, through a gas station old enough that you still need an actual key for the outside bathroom, and then we're on the road again, a shrink wrapped flat of bottled water squeaking awkwardly into the space between the front and back seats. I break the cap twisting it off, and spill some water in my lap, but then it's coursing over my lips and tongue and it's so sweet and cool and good, like I've never had water before in my life, only heard legends of it while I lived out in a desert. I drop the empty bottle between my feet and drink another one, a little slower but not by much, some dripping down my chin.

"Don't worry, I'm done," I say, before Dolly does anything to stop me from taking another.

"I'm sorry we can't give you more time," she says, in an uncharacteristically serious tone.

"We have the time we have," I say, feeling so detached from the world around me that in that moment I experienced no worry, no regret. I'm just not thirsty and have such a headache that all I can do is float in the timestream, since I'm not in the datastream.

And then there we are in a turnoff, waiting for the two transport vehicles to come down the road. Everything is flat, flat, but this seems to have been some kind of highway department maintenance site. Dolly does a final check of everybody's weapons and shoves a ballistic vest at Null. She's in her riot gear, and I'm in my riot gear, though I don't remember doing that when I got up this morning. There's a pole barn here, a few other buildings I can't really pinpoint the exact use of other than maybe storage or housing a water supply, and the hulking rusting out remains of a broken down snowplow. Both of our vehicles are visually hidden from the road, but Nicolai's car has a signal so we better hope DHS isn't running a scanner. I can only assume Nicolai has dragonscale, or a vest.

"You've done this before?" I ask Null as we get out our VR gear. Null's headset is practically factory stock, the kind a phone gets slotted into, little wireless keyboard in her hands.

"Hacked a vehicle? Yeah. Not one like this, though. It was a normal car. I did it just screwing around, seeing what could be done."

"It's a lot like that. Tougher security protocols, though. So if you can't get the one on your own, come and back me up, and we'll pair up to hit each one separately."

"Got it," Null says. She licks her lips, makes sure her earbuds are settled. She looks both nervous and excited, and I hope this isn't a huge mistake. Another huge mistake. There've been a few.

"All right then. We'll get our connections now, make sure we'll have control, and then do the hard shutdown when they're at that mile marker right there. Dolly and Nicolai will move in first, we'll make sure the communications stay down, and physically move in after."

Null looks at me a little oddly. "I got it. Dolly just went over it."

She did? "Just making sure. It doesn't hurt to be redundant."

"I'd rather hear it twice than mess up." She pulls her headset down.

There isn't much here that shows up in VR. There's an AR pinball machine booted up in the pole barn; must've been some kind of employee lounge. I can imagine snow plow guys hanging out there in shifts, sleeping on an old orange couch and just brewing pot after pot of coffee as the drifts keep piling up. It's kind of wild that the plow is still here, somebody could've stolen it and sold it for scrap by now. We could use it to block the road, interrupt the convoy, except they'd see it way too soon. My mind is caught on the plow, like when you bite the inside of your cheek and then bite the same place again over and over, accidentally. Or trip over the same spot in the sidewalk, the same break, even if you've been walking past it for years.

Dolly would love a snow plow plan. But a snow plow plan will get people killed. I don't say anything. Anyway, we have guns. I don't say anything.

//Can she handle a vehicle hack?// Dolly messages me. //Her goggles look like the kind of VR that grandmas get at the grocery store to play solitaire with.//

//She says she's done it before.// She'd hacked the same facility as me with those 'goggles', I don't remind Dolly.

Null and I virtually walk out to the mile marker where we want the vehicles stopped, past the ghostlike blips of Dolly and Nicolai's online equipment. And we wait. I watch the flagged vehicles come near, watch the little surveillance drones. These drones are automated and only record surveillance data, so that's good. The predators would have to deploy from a base, if the communications reached there. If. Which they won't, if we do our jobs. Normally I'm not worried. The walkies on all personnel rout through a dish on each vehicle, so if the vehicles are down, communications will be down.

I don't see anybody who looks like cybersecurity. I've got my VR in all around vision which I'll pay for later, the way I feel, but right now, I'm in it to win it. Bristol's in the second vehicle, I see now, but I'm in charge of the lead one. I prod the code gently, try the protocols I know already, run them through the dictionary hack program I modified for military hacks specifically, and after a moment I'm looking at the vehicle data. Personnel (female officer driving, three more men, one passenger side, two in back), weapons loadouts, GPS, connections to the base, destination coordinates. No place I recognize, I screencap it all and save it to search later. There's something throwing off a signal that I don't quite recognize, but it isn't communications and it isn't a weapon.

"You got it, Null?" I ask. This is a big ask for somebody we just met.

"I have it. You want to swap, so you've got her vehicle?"

"Yeah thanks." We do the handoff, and then I'm looking at the other vehicle's loadout. It's seriously different. All non-lethal, no repeat of that additional digital device, GPS tracker on Bristol. Probably her ankle. I got to work on that; Null had left it alone and I'm glad. On the walkies, I say "Kickoff in three, two, one," then I hit my virtual switch that ties everything in the targets together. Their satellite goes down, steering locks up, all of the engines slow. Front doors lock, Bristol's door unlocks, her GPS bracelet spoofing continued forward momentum. We'll have to manually remove it.

I steal a look at Null's work, for peace of mind I have to, but it's good. The vehicle stopped or is stopping, all of the doors locked, and as a bonus, the AR connection between their guns and their contact lenses are jammed. They might not even know it yet, that their biometrics and aim assists are off.

Distantly, I hear Dolly whooping. Nicolai's got to be with her, or covering the vehicles, or both. I watch everything that I switched off, that Null switched off, and so far everything's copacetic. So far, no other signals came online either, and I slide my headset up for a second to get a look at the real world, eyes squinted almost closed as I do.

The funny thing about bulletproof vehicle glass is it doesn't really shatter. The front passenger of vehicle one is hammering on their windshield with a gun butt, looks like, which when you think about it will screw up all their calibration even if Null hadn't already thrown them a whole bunch of static. The driver already has her seatbelt unfastened and is pretzeling herself around to try and kick out the windshield, I guess. Maybe she's yelling at him to help. It looks like she is. The first kick doesn't clear it and as she's crunching up for the second.

Nicolai stands with his weapon shouldered, just waiting for a target. Dolly's at the rear vehicle, already has Bristol out, and is fastening her in a bulletproof vest that makes her look like a woman in a business suit from the 1980s. Too big, but it'll stop what they're carrying, anyway. She isn't dressed in anything like her normal clothes. It looks a lot like hospital scrubs. And her hair is—

The windshield of the second vehicle is kicked out, and one of the guys slides off the hood and turns. Dolly extends the sawed off shotgun with just her right arm and squeezes off a round. It discharges with a weird noise that makes me think—hope—that Dolly loaded the beanbag rounds after all, and the guy folds up onto the pavement. The other one takes cover where I can't see, but Dolly's got her pistol out and uses the backseat as a step to hop up onto the roof of the car. She's practiced that. She walks on the roof to the front, aims down, and squeezes off three rounds, or maybe the pistol is a three round burst, I can't remember now. Is she whistling that song again? I have a feeling those are regular rounds. It seems like too little too late to be worried about shooting people, but I still feel a momentary twinge, a sudden big deep hollow in the pit of my stomach as things start to stretch out and slow down. And then Nicolai cries out and I turn to him like I'm underwater, like I'm dreaming.

He staggers back, clutching at his chest, but he's still standing. The vest took it. I've had bruises from being shot in armor before, but I'll take bruises over literal holes in me. I've never actually been shot in my flesh bits. Dolly has; she has a scar just under her right collarbone, and when Bristol exclaimed over it at first sight, Dolly had been super casual, saying if the bullet was bigger, or a little bit higher or lower, she would've ended up in a box. Or test driving one of those cybernetic arms so many people are excited about. Dolly has a lot of scars, and any explanation of them come with so much brag, there's no way to tell what's true and what Dolly's running her mouth over. Her arm though, her arm, and—

A bullet passes so close by my face I feel the air move as I stand there with my thoughts and my hand on my holstered gun, and that, *that* finally yanks me back to the real world with the fierce sharp focus of the combat adrenaline dump and that familiar drilling hot pain in my left temple. Null's running, though, Null tases the man from the front car, leaving him a jittering pile of person and equipment on the bumper of the car. I don't see the officer. The other two personnel from the front car are still in the back seat, still wrestling with seat belts and windows and bulky equipment, and trying to climb up front and also get out the windshield. The windshield trick is a good one; emergencies are varied, though. They take up a lot of brain space.

Dolly is yelling something, either at me or at Nicolai, or just yelling to yell. Null retreated again already, pulled her headset back down over her eyes. Then I see the officer.

That piece of equipment, that signal I couldn't figure out in virtual space, now it clicks into place. It's one of those proto-type cloaking devices, the next step up in camouflage gear, ex-cept it's too clunky, too expensive to produce in any kind of vol-ume. The officer, when she got out of the car, must've flipped the switch and then just flattened herself on the asphalt. Smart; the less varied the background, the better the device was going to be at replicating it. But the officer moved, not very much, but enough to maybe pull the rifle off the tased guy on the bumper, and my eye caught the shimmer in the air as the camo device tried to keep up with the movement. It's good, it's very good, but I just spent however long immersed in code, and when you're doing that you bet you keep your eye out all the time for irregularities like that when you're in VR immersion. I raise my gun and fire.

The device doesn't cloak the blood that spurts and begins pouring from that shimmery spot in the air. The device doesn't dampen the sound of the officer crying out in a cracked and raw-edged voice, and when she falls back, partly against the vehicle, the device can't track her movements as she thrashes in pain. For all that, I can't tell where I shot her, and I look around, sick and shaky, because there are at least two more guys I need to be worried about I think. It's not like me to lose track. It's *my job* to keep track.

Except there aren't any more, one already groaning and subdued, the other still enough that I assume he's dead. Dolly is a preternaturally good shot, and has joked more than once that she should just get a job in Vegas doing one of those old timey Wild West shows, except she'd be bored out of her skull and only be able to take it for so long.

I holster my pistol and leave it unsnapped, like I'm going to quick draw it or something if I need to. It's very quiet now, except for the officer's choked sobbing, her attempts to communicate with base. I have a quick peek in my headset and Null still has all comms locked down, including the little drones, which are resting now on the road. Dolly grinds one drone, then the other, under her boot heels as she clears weapons from the personnel, and then goes to the rear of the front car. "Pop the trunks," she says, calm as can be. Before I can do anything, Null has the trunk open, obscuring Dolly from view. Bristol stands off to the side, reloading a pistol. Nicolai stands next to her, quietly saying something, and Bristol looks at me for a moment before nodding, wavering a little on her feet.

Dolly pulls something the size of a cooler out of the trunk and hauls it over to the officer, who looks like she's glitching. It's like VR and the officer has something wrong with her code. I feel unsteady myself, but there's nowhere to sit down and we can't stay here. There's only so long we have before somebody comes looking for them. Dolly closes her eyes and feels around, and then the active camo switches off and the officer isn't a glitch anymore. She's a woman in cargos with a bullet proof vest and a sidearm, splattered with blood. My bullet went in above the vest, in that soft spot where the collarbones meet. I can't understand why she isn't dead already, because even though she's got a hand pressed on that spot, the blood's still pumping between her fingers. From the look on Dolly's face, she isn't really sure why either. But she rummages in the kit like she's going to try to help, and that's what unfreezes me.

I go to Dolly's side, drop down on my knees. The world does a too-far drop with me, shimmers at the edges, resolves. "What can I do? What are you going to do?"

"Well, they got this expanding foam that fills up wounds, that might do the trick. Or she might be done already. I'm no medic." Dolly breaks the top off the tube, shakes it briskly. "Gotta move your hand," she says to the officer, who looks up at her with glassy eyes and bloody foam flecking her lips, and for a second I think she's dead anyway. Then the officer moves her hand, eyes slipping closed, and Dolly sticks the nozzle against the wound and presses the button. It makes a noise like coating a slice of pie with whipped cream, and the foam is white. It reddens rapidly in spots, but the blood stops. Dolly picks up the officer's wrist, feels it for a moment. "Still hanging on." She pulls a pack of syrettes from the kit, separates one. "Painkillers," she says to me, and flicks the back of the officer's hand to make a vein stand out before sliding the needle in and depressing the plunger. The officer's face tightens, and then she relaxes on the ground.

"So I didn't kill her?"

Dolly blinks. "Not yet, anyway. Once we're ready to clear out, you can hit the big red panic button in their comms and medical will scramble for her." Dolly pulled a black box the size of a paperback book off of the officer's vest and hands it to me. "She's the only one wearing one of these, thank Christ. It's shitty, but still the best one of those we've seen yet."

"I've never seen—"

Dolly slaps the first aid kit closed and shoves that at me too, getting up. "Throw that in the Jeep. I figure you want to be out of here in ten, you think?"

"I think ten minutes might be too long," Bristol says from somewhere behind me. Maybe the other side of the car still.

"Five then, we're almost done." Dolly grabs me under the arm, pulls me up. "You okay?"

"Yeah." I'm not a new kind of not okay, anyway.

"The Jeep's just past the snow plow corpse," Dolly says. She pulls the officer's sidearm, picks up the rifle the officer had gone for. The tased guy is starting to recover, trying to close his twitching fingers on the rifle that isn't even there anymore. Like taking candy from a baby. What a weird saying that is. Who gives candy to babies anyway? "Grab one of the zip ties outta my pocket," she says to me, then she shakes her head. "Never-mind, go to the Jeep. Null!"

"I can do it," I say, but Null's doing it already, and then Dolly's got the guy face down on the asphalt next to the officer with his arms zip tied behind his back. "Now, it's not actually that hard to get out of zip ties," Dolly says. Nicolai comes, takes the first aid kit out of my hands. "You just gotta know the trick of it."

We stand, watching the guy a moment. "Which he doesn't," I say. Do I?

"Correct."

"Don't forget to pull their credentials," Bristol says over the headsets. Did Dolly give her earbuds already? Were hers just in her recovered belongings?

"You honestly think I'd forget a thing like that?" Dolly asks.

"Of course not," Bristol says with a laugh in her voice.

We're back at the Jeep and Nicola's car in four and a half minutes, dog tags and portable drives in a foil lined bag, active camo prototype in one of my cargo pockets. Null has her VR headset hung around her neck like me, keeps looking at the people, the cars, back to me every once in awhile, chewing her lip.

"What's up?" I ask. Bristol is in Nicolai's car, Dolly leaning in on the door and talking to her.

"I've never done anything like this before," Null says. "I've only ever just looked at things.

"We all start somewhere," I say, but I've never actually shot anybody before today. I've shot *at* them sure, but missed.

"I would dearly appreciate it if somebody would remove my unwanted accessory," Bristol says.

"Oh, sorry," I say. I should've been on that already. I grab my little tool case, crouch to look at the GPS tracker. I pull my headset up for a moment to make sure there isn't anything I'm missing, a dead man's switch or panic broadcast or I don't know what. We're so close. But it's clear. I shake the goggles up on my forehead and twist the final corrector, and the bracelet falls heavily to the ground.

"Alrighty then, back in the saddle, buckaroos," Dolly says. "Bitsy, just hop in here, Null come with me."

"Okay." When I'm not focusing on the job anymore I'm so exhausted I'm not sure I could've even walked to the Jeep. I crawl across the back seat of Nicolai's car. My ears are ringing, and I don't know when that started or if it will ever stop, and I just feel like I need to catch up with myself.

Bristol's kind of glassy eyed when she turns around to look at me, but I think that's from chemical restraints. "How do you like my hair?" she asks, running her hand over her buzzed scalp.

"Oh Bristol," I say, sad and sick. She always spends so much time on her hair. The whole package. Even in pajamas Bristol doesn't look as undone as she does now, so barefaced that it's like she's an unfinished painting.

"Bits, darling, you aren't crying are you? You aren't thinking about how limited by my hair I was! This is a stroke of genius, actually. Now I can look however I want. There are wigs in any style you can imagine. They really only helped me."

"Sure, it's like they set you free," Dolly says dryly over the headset. "It's ironic, just like that song."

"But the song—" I start to say, and Bristol laughs.

"Has been discussed to *death*," she says. I know the song but I don't know the song but who cares anyway. We saved Bristol, we did it. I don't know where we're going now. Dolly had a plan, did she tell me a plan? Wait I copied their maps.

"Bits." Dolly's been saying my name over and over for awhile, I guess. Trying to cut through the static.

"Yeah?"

"We're far enough out, call the ambos for them." Bristol is still looking at me and I slide the VR visor down so I don't have to think about what look should be on my face. I lie back on the plush leather of the back seat. We've covered more miles already than I realize, and the connection is choppy, but I delete the code that brought down the convoy's communications, hit their panic button for emergency services.

"Done."

Nicolai is being awfully quiet. I wonder why. Probably starting to feel the bruises under his vest.

"Roger that," Dolly says cheerfully. Bristol should've gone in her Jeep, they could've gossiped about me all they needed to without bothering me about it. Nicolai turns on the radio, or maybe Bristol does, some kind of old but new techno jazz, instrumental. I could sleep forever, I think. But no, of course I can't, the rocking car stops soothing me after awhile and starts making me feel like I'm gonna throw up.

"Who's our new friend?" Bristol asks quietly when I sit up and pull my visor off. Her hand is on the walkie mute.

"We picked her up earlier," I say, not sure if that's right, but Nicolai doesn't say no. "She was hacking the same place I was, at the same time, and they caught her."

"Convenient," Bristol says.

"Bristol, she's just a kid," I say. But should I have thought about this more? Dolly should've thought about it more, anyway. I have been unwell.

"I'm sure it's fine."

"She's been very helpful," Nicolai offers.

"Especially when nobody else was, I imagine," Bristol says.

"We tried to..." I trail off. I don't need to tell her this. Walkie channels open again, I say "I hope we're finding a place to hunker down."

"Just putting some pavement between us and them, and then yeah, we'll find another off the beaten path gem like the ones we've been purveying. Sorry Nicky."

"It's to be expected," he says.

Chapter Fourteen

I didn't know so many motels with burned out signs and un-paved driveways existed, and yet here we are again. Dolly has a special knack for finding them, I guess, the way Bristol can always find a place to eat that serves authentic espresso. Weird little not quite superpowers, and I try to think about what I think mine is and think about Null saying I was a VR legend. Dolly and Nicolai go off to get food before we think about what that kind of decision might mean for the rest of us, and Bristol gets in the shower. She has a bag that Dolly must've got-ten for her from a bus station locker. I must've lost time again, blanked out during that stop.

Null sits cross-legged on one of the beds, pretending to look intently at her screen. She looks at me sometimes, looks away. She wants to talk about what happened today and I want to do that for her, be a mentor or whatever, and I can't. I'm ly-ing flat on the bed on my back and the bed still feels like the car on the road. I curl over on my side again and just hope that it'll stop before I have to go in the adjoining room and throw up. Dolly left the connecting door open, anyway. My head hurts and doesn't hurt, sometimes fine, sometimes like my skull is a butterfly tacked to velvet, like my headache is a dying fluores-cent bulb. I try to decide which it'll stop on, when the flickering stops, hurting or not. It used to be not. Hurts me, hurts me not.

Then Dolly and Nicolai are back, Dolly's boots untied again somehow, if she ever tied them in the first place, talking too loud for me to sort words and I just shove my head harder against the pillow. Dolly clomping out again, coming back as Bristol exits the bathroom in a cloud of steaming rose scent. "They're out of fucking ice, can you believe it?"

"I'm amazed they provide the illusion of having ice to begin with," Bristol says, like a cartoon cat who doesn't like getting her paws wet.

"What do we need ice for?" I ask, sitting up, regretting it.

"Your head and the warm booze Nicky had in his trunk," Dolly says, looking at me critically. "We should take the party into the other room."

"Maybe it'll help if I eat," I say. It never helps when I eat.

We eat—well they eat—and somebody puts on old movies on the crappy motel network. Probably Bristol. Black and white old movies, not even early aughts.

"So what now?" I ask. "We got Bristol out, we all go home now?" Bristol shoots Dolly an accusing look.

"Not exactly," Dolly says. That sparkle's still in her eyes.

"What do you mean?" I say at the same time as Bristol says "You didn't tell her?"

Dolly sighs, elaborately. Nicolai looks uncomfortable, or maybe he just never looks comfortable, and I look at Null, who is just watching and listening avidly, like she's taking notes.

"Every time I tell her it doesn't work," Dolly says.

"How can it 'not work', what does that mean?"

"It means it doesn't work, she just can't." Dolly kind of flaps a hand and finishes her drink. "She can't hear it without like, rebooting."

"Rebooting?" Bristol's staring at me now, her eyes luminous under too much forehead. There wasn't a wig in that bag Dolly brought, even if there were clothes and cosmetics and rose scented shower stuff. There probably aren't wig vending machines.

"She tries to tell me some things, and I hear white noise, and then wake up again doing something else." I wait, but for once, Bristol has nothing to say. Maybe she's still coming off the drugs they were giving her. She probably shouldn't be drinking, but it's too late now.

"Dolly, you can't expect her to *work* like this!"

"I did just fine," I say. I did a good job. I also just want to go someplace dark and sleep for a thousand years, so why should I even argue about this? I should just say I can't do it. Mission accomplished.

"You did, Bits, there's no faulting your work. I only mean—"

"I know what you mean," I say. She stops talking and quirks her lips, glances at Dolly. "Okay. Tell me the story again."

"I thought you just said hearing the story reboots you?" Bristol asks. Dolly's looking at me though, squinting just a little.

"Something changed," she says. Not really a question.

"I think maybe," I say, thinking of the dream with the wall coming down. Maybe my subconscious is running its own dictionary hack. "How's the arm?"

"Purring like a kitten," she says, flashing a grin. She pauses, nods, hands me the tequila. "Okay."

"Okay," I say, and swig from the bottle. I always forget, tequila isn't my favorite.

"So we were tracking down the leads on some of our diamond data. Looking at the older cold war stuff, the stuff we thought had to be decommissioned. And we found a program that sounded really familiar. To me, anyway."

"Why would you know anything about a program?" I ask. I take another swig of the tequila, hold up the bottle to look at the scorpion in the bottom, its tail half curled. It looks like it has little hairs on its claws, but they're probably called something other than hair.

"Not a computer program, darling," Bristol says. I wonder if she knows she's touching her head behind her ear, where hair would've been, but every one of Bristol's gestures is on purpose.

"More like project, I guess," Dolly says. She keeps looking at me, waiting for me to static out and reboot. I'm in kind of a neutral state, no real headache though I'm sure it's waiting, no white noise whine in my ears, though I'm sure it's waiting too. "Way back then they didn't really have cybernetics yet, just the ideas of it. From crazy scientists, I guess, and books and movies. But like, the Russians have almost always had the idea of super soldiers, right? And America never likes being beat out by anybody, much less the Russians."

"But this was Russian intel." I had the diamond data all backed up; normally I could search it up quicker than they could explain it to me.

"Russian intel about an American program."

"An ongoing American program," I say, without realizing I was going to say it.

Dolly nods eagerly. "At a lot of sites across the country, most of which are decommissioned."

"So we were looking for the places that were payday versus actual live fire engagement," I say. I'm remembering, not-re-membering. I can't remember what comes next until I say it, like rereading a book that I last saw when I was three. There's something I'm forgetting, something Dolly doesn't want to say in front of Null, or maybe she's just trying to feel out where the new boundary of my difficulty is. Same.

"We were, yeah. And some of 'em, I knew about and some I didn't and we were mapping it out and matching things to-gether. We were kinda looking for the one that I remembered. For something more, um, personal. Than just a payday."

"The one you...remembered." I wasn't feeling so great any-more. I wasn't holding the bottle anymore, Bristol had it, though she definitely hated tequila and only drank it if the so-cial situation required. Dolly didn't notice, either deliberately or because she's Dolly.

"Lots of places, the government, or I guess maybe it was private corporations on government contract, brought in locals to work on. Promised them a paycheck, that their families would be looked after. By then, that was the only chance some of those locals had at a future, and they took that chance."

"You were one of them."

"Me. My brother. Some of our friends." She takes the bottle from Bristol, takes a swig. "Some of us, by the time we were done, were sent off to other places, and mostly didn't know what happened to each other."

"So is this a payday or revenge?"

"Both. Neither. Ain't nobody gonna feel bad for what they did to us. Hell, I mostly feel fine about it, physically. It's the rest of it that I got the problem with." Weirdly, I remember her talking about bees. Corporations and their bees, locals and their bees. It's hard to imagine Dolly as a farmer, a beekeeper, anything than what she is now. What is she now? What am I?

They keep talking but the static overtakes me like an avalanche, like the ocean, and I'm pulled under.

Chapter Fifteen

I dream of the hot green seething trees around my villa, that encased it in flickering shadows even at noon. I dream of tigers. Tiger cubs, playing in the clearing just down the hill, where the old owner landed helicopters. Fully grown tigers, and they're normally solitary, aren't they? Nosing open the door, once it rained enough, and dried enough, and the door swelled off its hinges and my sad eyed real estate agent couldn't find a new buyer. Tigers prowling in the hallways, maybe pursuing rodents, catching mice, like if people hunting for potato chips was a thing.

I walk past the tigers in the hall, to my VR immersion room, to find the server stacks intact again, the hard drives in place, LEDs blinking briskly. And I'm there in the chair again, all of the little pads connected, the mesh over my head for the neurological impulses, the visor over my eyes, the IV settled in my arm. I stand over myself, looking down. Looking at the displays on the machines. Looking at my immersion-slack face, not so different from sleep, I guess. And then, as I watch, rivulets of blood began to come from my nose, and from my eyes beneath the visor, from the corner of my mouth.

Then there's a grumbling in the room, the chuffing, coughing noise that tigers make, and one pushes me aside, pushes standing awake-me aside, and goes to prone VR-immersed-me and begins to lick the blood off my face. But a tiger's tongue is very rough, rough enough to lathe flesh from bones, and so my face begins to come off, in blood dripping layers, the VR visor clattering to the arm of the chair and then the tiled floor, dragging on the end of its cable, the mesh hanging up in the tiger's teeth until it chuffs again, face and nose wrinkled, and tugs it away. The tiger keeps licking and my skin keeps coming off.

When I come fully awake, I'm almost on my feet in the now-dark hotel room, the sheets and blankets tangling me up. Mostly dark, the blue-gray light of dawn seeping around the window shades. Somebody has their hands on my shoulders...Bristol. She's saying something, maybe I'm saying something, everything is white noise and bright lights in the corners of my vision where I'm sure no lights are on. I sit down on the bed so abruptly that Bristol stumbles, shoulders into me, the most graceless thing I've ever seen her do. Then she sits on the bed next to me, breathing hard. Dolly stands in the doorway between rooms, sawed-off shotgun in hand, adjoining room lit behind her and Nicolai saying something in Russian that I can't sort out. Or don't I speak Russian?

"Bitsy what the fuck?" Dolly says.

"I had a bad dream," I say, which seems so childish and stupid. My mouth has the heavy copper taste of blood in it, and my face is wet, but when I wipe it, no blood comes away on my hands, they're just wet from tears, sweat.

"I can see that," she says. She flicks the safety on the shotgun, which strikes me as really funny. Sawed off shotgun, but with a safety. But I can't find the energy to laugh, and also probably that's good because it would be far more alarming if I just start laughing now. In the dim room I can see the orangey striped tiger, the blood blotting out the white between the black stripes. I can hear the heavy tearing sound of its tongue lathing, the rain-like patter of blood on the floor. I shudder, and Bristol shifts, seems to hesitate, and puts an arm around me. Dolly comes and sits on the other side of me, does the same thing.

"I've never heard you make a noise like that before, Bits," Bristol says.

"I'm sorry," I say. I'm still crying, I realize. Just seeping tears. Tears, not blood, hot on my face.

Dolly kind of gives me a squeeze. "Nah, we needed a wake-up call at dawn anyway, more or less. This way we can get all situated and ready to roll out. Sound good?"

"Yeah," I say, a few moments of sorting out Dolly's sudden shift into businesslike. Maybe not so sudden. Maybe Dolly hadn't actually been sleeping, and was just mentally running the scenario all night. That is very much like her. And this is honestly the most I've seen Dolly care about something, the most sustained focus I've seen her give something. Even after the diamond heist, she'd been more relaxed. Though 'relaxed Dolly' is still also 'ready to spring into action Dolly'. Like a tiger lounging in the sun.

"Was it a VR dream?" Null asks quietly. I'd forgotten about her.

I hesitate. "More or less." I wipe my face again. "I dreamed about Mexico, and tigers. At my place there."

"Mexico," Null says, in a musing tone.

"She had herself set up in an old drug lord's villa," Dolly says, her voice light and easy as always. "Problem is, there were rumors the guy had pet tigers that he just turned loose before he bugged outta there. Probably just rumors. But enough to make you wanna carry a gun all over the place."

"Tigers? Yeah, wow. That's scary."

"I never saw one," I say. "Or even heard one. It probably wasn't true."

"Probably," Dolly agrees. "But clearly it's a risk you were willing to take."

"Clearly." I squeeze my eyes shut, open them again, hoping to banish the afterimages of stripes, luminous eyes, white whiskers turning red. "Is it okay if I take the first shower?"

"Of course," Bristol says.

Hot water is a mistake, all of my sinuses throbbing like I've been beaten about the head. Cold water has its obvious downsides too, but I chatter my way through a thorough scrub down anyway, my head in such crystalline pain that I think it'll shatter at any second. But now I can think straight, at least for those seven minutes, and I think of whatever decommissioned site we're going to down in Louisiana, a part where hardly anybody lives anymore after hurricane after hurricane came roaring up through, Cat 5 and bigger, levies gone, cities gone, so much overrun swampland and forest. So much kudzu. So many feral hogs. It's the perfect place to keep going with clandestine stuff, especially if you're picking your 'volunteers' from a population where doctors are scarce and you have families needing to be seen to.

We pack everything in the Jeep, everybody in the Jeep, except for Nicolai. "Decided not to come with us after all?" I ask.

"I have a different role," he says.

"Safer, and yet somehow more lucrative," Bristol says. "Not that we lack for funds, mind," she hurries to add. She isn't used to my being confused all the time, missing information. Join the club.

"It was a pleasure spending time with each of you," Nicolai says stiffly.

He drives away before we do, and it's hard for me to not just keep tabs on his vehicle. But I don't want him backtraced if our operation goes sideways, again, and I uncouple his walkie from our network and try to put him out of my mind.

We make a couple of stops, bathroom breaks, breaks to get out of the car and walk around and stretch, so Bristol and Dolly can get away from each other for five minutes. One of the rest stops has a wifi booster, and I make short work of their security, slapping my VR headset on and getting right down to the fiber optic connection like somebody coming out of the desert going for their first drink of water. Apparently I've searched for super soldier black sites before, but not in conjunction with Louisiana, and I do another broad search, file grab everything I can find to scan through when the connection drops again. I toe into the dark net for information too, though what I immediately find looks like a lot of tinfoil hat nonsense. Still, I grab that too, because who knows where I'm going to find some truth, something to tease out of the wreckage of human reasoning and follow to a useful source.

I pull off my VR headset at the same time Null is doing the same. "Hey, let me look at your setup. I told you I would."

"Thanks." Null hands it over almost shyly.

It's matte black plastic; most of this stuff is, not unlike the active camo box that I've still got in my pocket. I should give that to Dolly. There's black electrical tape reinforcing some of the seams where the thing's been pried open, probably to add more RAM, a bigger processor, things that even an out-of-the-box unit purely for kids to play video games on won't have, but can accommodate. It's a bitch getting everything to fit back together, I remember that from my first one. Everybody remembers their first VR headset, pried apart, cobbled back together, tool-scored, tape-gummed, with its occasional hitches and starts in processing, a troublesome proclivity to disconnect and power cycle if you didn't get the soldering just right. The head strap is some kind of web material, an imitation of what military belts and straps were made out of, comfortable enough for awhile, but also the kind of thing that lets the buckles slip their adjustments incrementally as time goes by.

I run my thumbnail under the tape, find the tabs, pop it open. The soldering jobs are very good, actually, and all the components more or less jigsawed together just as one would like. The RAM's a little wiggly, and there are two cut rate graphics cards working together to try and do the work of a midrange one. The heat sinks are well placed, and the fans (because there are fans and not a liquid cooled system) are very small, really smooth running. I look at them, try to figure what kind of equipment they'd been pulled from. Maybe a video game console, maybe some kind of remote kids toy like a robot or a drone.

"Hardware looks pretty good, considering," I say.

"My budget screwed me, of course," Null says with a shrug.

"That's how it is for all of us. But you do really well with your equipment, which means you'll be amazed at what you can do with a decent headset, something that's better out of the box before you make your adjustments. Which, again, are very good."

"Thanks," Null says, and she's a little pink on the edges again, though this time from pride, I think, not embarrassment.

"It's okay if I test drive it?" I ask. She already said so, but it's just what you do. The etiquette of looking over other people's equipment.

"Yeah, go right ahead." Null's pretty good at sounding casual, but I can only think of the first time I had an older veteran hacker who was willing to look over my rig. It was nerve wracking and exciting, and I wanted both to get complimented and to get pointers on how to get past whatever bugs were hindering me, the hang-ups I still had no matter how much I'd tinkered and scanned and adjusted.

I slip the headset on, boot it up. Even on my head, the fans are very quiet. Maybe the kid likes the fans, maybe it's a budget thing. I'll bring up closed system liquid cooling; it's less able to be interfered with by random signals, or magnets or whatever. Not all that hard to do, either, with a couple of parts.

Connectivity out here is bad in the first place, but Null's signal is strong, then rapidly declines, and then spikes again, something my rig isn't doing. Something I could probably adjust, maybe something I could replace from my kit of assorted tools and parts, the stuff you keep around just in casies. I don't have a viable replacement for the video chip, nothing that would fit in Null's differently shaped headset, and that's a shame. The colors are a little off, but I'm not sure if that's a settings issue, Null's preference, or just my brain going weird again.

I do some general internet things, check movie times in Los Angeles, look at the space elevator construction webcam.

There's a sandstorm in Dubai, obscuring most of the camera view, but I can still see the bright yellow construction vehicles, their headlights piercing the gloom.

I pull up maps, pick a random location, Seattle, and walk around for a few minutes in the VR. Null doesn't have the all-around vision toggled, opting for 180 instead. Even with the headset, the feedback is good, the sense of walking motion appropriate, not mismatched. It's raining in Seattle, because of course it is, and I don't opt to pull the available umbrella. Cold raindrops fall on my scalp, on my shoulders, but the rain feeling isn't quite right, and that's the fault of the haptics. I open a few more things and then stream a music video too while all of it's going, and there's some sluggishness, some hitches, more of those spikes and lags. The wiggly RAM tries like hell to do its job, but I wouldn't run like that any longer than I had to.

I shut down what I opened, pull the headset free of my head, take a second to acclimate to the world around me, the sunlight.. "It's good, overall," I say. "Most of your problems are hardware, like I said. Have you thought about liquid cooling?"

"Of course I've thought about liquid cooling, who hasn't? But you see the space I'm working with, and the odds and ends I have jammed in there, those little fans were the best I could do for the time being. If I could get liquid cooling—"

"You could improve the video card, and then I think there would be space for you to improve the haptics too." I don't mention the connectivity spikes. I have a weird feeling that I don't know how to address.

"Oh hell yeah!"

"You nerds," Dolly says with a laugh. I jump. I forgot we were all in the Jeep together. "You're all the same."

Chapter Sixteen

We're in Louisiana and kind of circling around to where we want to go, or to Dolly wants me to go, before she sends me a file. God knows where she stores anything, and I didn't know she had any wireless storage on her. Maybe she just keeps it in an envelope until she needs it, pulls it out, puts it away again. It makes sense that she didn't give it to me before now, I probably couldn't have handled it.

I lost time again; Bristol is wearing a wig that she didn't have before, gleaming auburn like one of the foxes in my painting, sleek and straight and probably just long enough to put up in the French twist that she likes so much, if you can do things like that with a wig. I have no idea.

There's fast food bags on the seats between me and Null, and drinks in the holders. Mine is the iced coffee, I assume, and when Dolly glances back, sees that I'm with the world again, she reaches down in the console between her and Bristol, pulls out a rattling white bottle, and tosses it to me. "Got some good stuff," she says. "Proceed with caution."

When did she get some good stuff? Where? "Thanks," I try to read the label and my eyes just slide right off the teeny tiny words and numbers, and I finally just take one, my iced coffee really more lukewarm by this point and I wonder why until I look out the window at the not-quite-paved-anymore road, the huddled green forms of what were once houses overgrown with trees and bushes and kudzu, grasses so long that they bend and mat together under their own weight. It's the kind of grass you'd want a machete to walk through, both to clear a path and to fend off, I don't know, wildlife. Poisonous snakes and feral hogs and whatever other dangers were in the used-to-be inhabited deep south. People still live here, in places, I know that. But they're the kind of people who decided they didn't want to leave their land, they didn't want to move into the suburbs, or the cities, and deal with everything that entailed. Population and surveillance and police and the constant inundation of advertising and news. I mean, I ignore a lot of those things pretty well, even when I'm not on-purpose getting around them in ways that said police would be less than happy to know about. My own version of roughing it; inhabiting the modern world, but embracing the digital beyond what most normal citizens ever do. A step beyond, not a step back. "How much longer? Do you want to tell me, so I can try and check it out?"

"Couple hours, maybe, depends on the roads." She glances at Bristol, or maybe me; hard to tell with her sunglasses. Is she hesitating, or concentrating on the road? Is she hesitating because of Null? Dolly never hesitates. And what's *my* problem with Null? She's just a wet-behind-the hacker ears hacker kid who got into a target way over her head. "We're making a rest stop at the next likely place, though."

"That's good." I feel like so much of the last...week? Has it been a week? Has been made up of rest stops and driving and drinking various things and then having to stop again. Maybe it's the normal amount of stops and I just didn't notice before, my head in VR all the time, sifting through files, surveilling the sites and likely sites, getting a sense of what we needed to avoid in order to all come away from it successful and alive. We'd had such a good record of that until whatever screwed up my head.

The gas station isn't really a gas station anymore, so Dolly almost drives past it, until Bristol says "They do have lights on. And an open sign." She pulls the Jeep around and parks, and cuts the engine, and we all get out and stretch. It's the time of year when everything seems to be more green than anything real could be, and bugs I don't know the names of scream in chorus from the grass, and from the trees. Cicadas, some of them, I'm sure. It must be a nightmare trying to keep this patch of land clear, whether they intend it to be a parking lot anymore or not. Everything grows aggressively right up to the edges, and there's grass and Queen Anne's Lace shoving up through cracks in the pavement. There's a barbecue grill off to one side, but I don't smell anything cooking.

"Well let's just hope they're friendly," Dolly says. Null, almost to the door, pauses like it hadn't occurred to her that they might not be. Dolly laughs. "I'm sure they're friendly, kiddo, it's okay. I even left the AK in the Jeep."

"The AK?" Null asks and I think, hasn't Null seen it? Why didn't Dolly use it when we hijacked Bristol's captors? But I guess that would've been dumb. It's not a weapon known for its accuracy. Dolly just laughs again and kind of claps Null on the shoulder and walks into the place without taking her sunglasses off like she's a movie badass, and we trail in behind her. Bristol comes last, doing some fiddly thing with her makeup in a little compact mirror. If I didn't know it was a wig, I wouldn't know it was a wig.

There's a guy kind of near the counter, and two just-older-than toddlers playing with toys near the back, and his smile doesn't seem too guarded when the little bell rings over the door and we all walk in. I wonder when his last customers came through. I wonder how he gets supplies. From people like us, probably. I get a not quite memory, an echo, a digital ghost, of Dolly talking about hijacking autodriving eighteen wheelers out on a highway someplace. Salt. I remember doing that.

"Bathroom?" Dolly asks before any pleasantries are exchanged, and he smiles a little and points, and we split off to browse. Just like civilization. The kids don't really pay us any attention; either they're too absorbed in their game, or they were really drilled not to talk to strangers. I look for digital signatures in AR, a wireless booster, cameras, even just a cell phone, and I don't see any of that. Not like my internet connection is great, but it's still there. Thanks SpaceX.

I find some coffee drinks I've never heard of and the caffeine can really only help at this point. Weirdly, they have a display of the types of brain vitamins I'm supposed to have been taking, and I grab a couple of bottles. Do I have cash? I poke around in my pockets and find some rumpled up bills, their little holo-AR numbers jumbled and pixelated. In a city they might not even take these, but here, the guy behind the counter doesn't even blink, just counts and counts me back my change.

There's a broken-down lottery ticket machine, and after I take my vitamins, I kind of lean on that while I wait for everyone, with an area map pulled up in AR. It's looking familiar, based on some of those maps that I pulled when I grabbed a bunch of those military files, and I start flicking through those, looking for the one that I remembered.

Distantly, I hear Dolly's laugh, loud and brash as always, and think we're probably about to leave. We should be. It's like I can feel a clock on us now, an urgency to get this done. I find the map I remembered and it isn't quite the same as here, but it's close, and I wonder if it's pre-the last biggest storm. I overlay the two, wiggle them around. It's possible the place we want is underwater now. It's possible it's one of those kudzu mummies off on a road that isn't a road anymore, all the trees swathed in Spanish moss and alligators sunning themselves on the broken up driveways. Maybe there are cougars or panthers or whatever; didn't there used to be wildcats here? Well, Dolly has an AK. I've got a gun. Bristol...well I guess she'll need a gun 'cause she's unlikely to just Disney princess charm animals into not attacking us.

I save my work, close the windows. It might be the caffeine mega dose, might be the vitamins, might be the good stuff, might be wishful thinking, but I feel like my headache is diminished. I feel more normal. Or maybe I just think I feel more normal? There are so many variables at play. I see Null giving me what I think is kind of a weird look but think no, she probably either isn't looking at me at all or her look is entirely normal.

And then she glances away when I notice, so it was definitely a weird look.

Then I think of a saying in our circles, that it isn't paranoia if somebody is actually after you.

It'd be stupid to assume people *weren't* after us, after what we pulled last year. Maybe Null is part of a team watching for us to resurface.

We're walking back out to the Jeep, Bristol still chattering, Dolly laughing once in awhile, and I'm thinking that Null's headset really only needs to connect to the internet and VR in the most basic of ways, and if she's on their side, whoever they is, homeland, or whatever, they can just give her signal all the permissions she needs. She doesn't really need to hack anything, and that leaves room for her equipment to—no, I looked at her equipment, there was nothing weird in there. Nothing I haven't seen before. But her connection fluctuating like that, it meant something and I knew it but I didn't know *what* it meant. Except that she's been with us for days now and very definitely knows who we are and whoever she's working with knows exactly all of that as well.

Without thinking, I purse my lips and whistle that little tune that Dolly's been repeating since she woke me up. Dolly's head whips around like she's a dog who just heard the treat bag rattle, and our eyes lock. I tilt my head, just a little, at Null, who's walking just ahead of me. Dolly gives the barest of nods, and she and Bristol climb into the Jeep first. I can only hope that they have a rapid furtive conversation before Null and I get there, and that they clue me in. We're in the final approach, and we've had to handle this kind of thing before, but I can't imagine we're going to get away with it as easily as we did with Will.

Chapter Seventeen

I send Nicolai a message to warn him. It's bad luck, that every time we need help beyond the three of us, we've been compromised. Marquis, I think, ended up with a very good deal, and is safe and happy somewhere, but they probably would've been safer and happier right where they were in the first place. At least Nicolai was actually kind of in this life to begin with. It wasn't entirely our fault.

Null hadn't sent out any messages since we stopped, that I noticed. How many did she send out before? Did she just have a constant screen-shared connection with handlers at some HQ? Was there a satellite HQ, a roving van that hovered closer to us than we ever would've considered, ready to swoop in and...arrest us. I guess. Take us away to a place like where they had Bristol, where nobody would know, and nobody would care what happened to us, as long as they got "results" for whatever actual government agencies—not shadow agencies—they reported to.

And like, I'm not confused that they consider us criminals, of course we are. But legitimate lives were long-ago made too small to be bearable and this is what we chose for ourselves instead. But it doesn't mean we're not still *people*. It doesn't mean I don't believe in a little thing called human rights.

Oh wouldn't that stick it to them, if I backtraced Null and blew their operation open by leaking it all to a legitimate news source. People who operated from physical studios, and who had money and clout and public support. I could only assume it was the same government agency (but name undisclosed, wink wink) that helped us out with the diamonds thing, who we then double crossed, which was mostly Bristol's doing but it's not like we three didn't all agree to the idea. We had our cake and ate it too, some faster than others. I take a sec, check my accounts; yeah, I've still got money left, in the ballpark of what I thought I did. I check in on Null's activity again. She tried to trace what I was doing, I think, but still hasn't unsnarled my vpn, my proxy servers, my reroutes. She just knew I was connected to the internet, and that there was activity on my connection. I cycle my passwords, because fuck her dictionary hack if she's running one, and I try to focus on a plan. A plan for whatever this location is, and for dealing with Null.

I imagine Dolly would have a very succinct suggestion for dealing with Null. Maybe it'll come to that, maybe it won't. It didn't with Will. She suggested it then, for sure, and Bristol smoothed it out instead. Dolly always likes simple, though. It's not that I don't like simple; I just understand that it doesn't always work out like that.

I also understand that I probably haven't chased away the headache forever, especially if whatever's wrong with me isn't to do with just being in VR for six months, but to do with whatever cost Dolly her arm. Or did that happen even longer before that? I don't have that information at hand in my brain. I could message one of them and ask. We've got enough to worry about.

We roll down green tunnels of country road with Dolly and Bristol bickering pleasantly in the front seat. I sigh and lean back in my seat, slide my VR headset on. Null doesn't say anything, has been quiet since the last rest stop, actually. Maybe furiously making final plans with her handlers or whatever. Maybe just tired. Maybe not a spy after all. Guess I'll find out.

Because of Null's lag spikes, she doesn't even notice me waltzing into her system. Or if she does, she's better than I'd thought. You judge a person on their equipment, you have to, and what if she was a tried and true professional and embarrassed to be running the rig she had, not proud that she accomplished as much with so little? Too many options. I don't read people face to face good enough for this, that's Bristol's job. Even Dolly's better at it than I am. I poke around in her task manager for a screen sharing app, a direct uplink app, anything like that, and I find both. Great. Jesus I wish I was in my right mind. I backtrace, save the IP address elsewhere in my systems so I can revisit it later. I have to cut her connection. I have to tell Bristol and Dolly that I'm doing it, and why. Beyond that, I don't want any decisions to be up to me.

It is and isn't an easy thing, planting malicious code. It's harder with another hacker who's seasoned, but it's easier if they're using unfamiliar equipment, and equipment that's deliberately lowballing their abilities.

Her stuff doesn't black out immediately; I want it to do a slow fade, kind of mimicking her spikes, until after one of the low times when the connection bottoms out, it just doesn't come back. Weirdly specific, I guess, but I already have a little program that does close to that. I make the necessary tweaks and take a minute to flick through her file registry, what little there is of it. She doesn't even have any *music*, I really definitely should've known. I set the program running, then message Dolly and Bristol: //Null is a plant, I don't have full info yet but I'll bet her people and Will's people are pretty close. I'm cutting her headset's capabilities, she'll probably squawk about that pretty soon. Not sure how much damage she's done.//

It's a fun little program, actually, malicious without actually hurting anything. It isn't ransomware, and all your files are still there. You just can't connect to the internet for awhile. It times itself out again over seventy two hours, or can just be deleted from the registry, if you can find it. If you can tell it apart from all of the other legit registry programs that it ghosts itself to look like.

I back off my connection with Null's headset, and not long after hear her cry of dismay, that kind of soft, frustrated noise we all make when technology stops working but, by all rights, it should be working. Or it was working and now isn't and you didn't do anything. Should I check out that IP now? Maybe not. I pull my headset down, so it's around my neck and I almost don't have to squint, the tree cover is so thick. "What happened?"

"I've got nothing here. Are you still okay?" Null has her headset in her hands, the reset button held down.

"I was, yeah. Not great, but had a couple bars." I pull my headset up again like I'm checking, and I do check for new connections, for drones, lurking vehicles or what have you. We're clear. "Yeah, still operational."

"What the *hell*," she mutters. I wonder how old she really is, if she's working with a government agency. Most of the people we saw last year were so *young*, or maybe they just all look young, and do those rich-people fountain of youth blood transfusions or something. Wouldn't that be a hook, live forever, just work for this shadow agency. Government vampires.

"Bits?" Dolly actually sounds worried. I blink and the Jeep is stopped. She's turned around in the driver's seat, one hand still on the wheel, seatbelt straining. Even Dolly still wears her seatbelt.

"Yeah, yeah, I'm okay, sorry. Got sleepy I guess," I say lamely. I only lost about twenty minutes this time but I guess I was pretty far gone. Bristol is turned around too, actually. Null's attention is split about 70/30 between her headset and me. It occurs to me that I should've assumed she had contact lenses too, but it doesn't seem to be the case. She'd be blinking alternately, I think, or rubbing at her eyes, if not outright just touching her eyeball to shift the lenses. Ask me how I know. Just thinking about it makes me blink a little more. I'm sure that's not reassuring to Dolly. "Are we there yet?"

"Not yet," Dolly says, a frown briefly quirking her lips, furrowing her brow.

"I'm fine," I say, eyes wide and earnest even as I'm starting to see flickers in my peripheral vision, because I'm fine right now, that's the truth. It'd be really nice to have a good twelve hours without a migraine. Without a headache. Maybe we can get through this. Once I get through this I can sleep for another six months, and I'm more than starting to think that the long VR time isn't the problem here. "Let's get this show on the road."

"Sure thing," Dolly says, putting the Jeep in gear again, though Bristol looks at me longer.

"We'll have a spa day after this," Bristol says in a voice that's a particular sort of kind-but-critical, the voice that says I don't drink nearly enough water, nor moisturize my skin enough.

"Sure thing," I say. It wouldn't be terrible. There are worse things.

Chapter Eighteen

We get closer to Dolly's undisclosed location and Null gets more frustrated with her equipment. She tries to hide it, increasingly badly. I'm not sure what's occupying Bristol's thoughts at this time; for all I know, she's catching up on social media scandals that occurred for...however long she was incarcerated. I saw it in her file, but my mind slides away from it like trying to read in a dream, so I let it go. She's here, she's fine. She's a better liar than all of us, but we never lie to each other. She's fine.

I slide my headset on, double check my proxies, and then go investigate the address of whoever was attached to Null's headset when I torpedoed the connection. I'm sure they're on high alert. I would be. They don't know if she lost connection just because of where we are; the hurricane-ravaged south that has little left in the way of infrastructure except i pockets where some people decided to fancily and flashily rebuild, with habitats and seawalls and other high tech weather resilient structures. Only certain types get in, of course; those who can afford to live there, and those who get paid to work there.

But Null's people haven't sent any response yet, if they even intend to. There aren't any active drones in our proximity, there's no police who have peeled off from their regular patrols and are inbound. I'm sure whoever Null was reporting to is still sitting in their cushy neo cold war bunker and trying to raise the connection, maybe trying to access any local cameras to see where we've gone, maybe trying to connect with a satellite to focus on our location, but good luck with all the tree cover and the off-green Jeep that Dolly had to've picked for exactly this reason.

She did; I'm staring at code and then I've got a flash of memory, a waking dream, her and I in a used car lot where somehow the guy only had dialup and was more than willing to take the cash that she counted out to him. Broken pavement and faded plastic garlands of flapping flags, gray sky, broken glass right in against the curbs, like that's as far as they swept it and there was no point trying to do anything more, a quarter machine full of little white squares of gum that were rock hard and didn't even smell minty anymore. The salesman whose voice was too loud when it didn't need to be, whose suit was more expensive than it needed to be. He was the only one there, did all the paperwork himself on a typewriter that was older than all three of us put together. Faxed it off to nowhere, for all I know, on a machine that wheezed and screamed like the phone line was haunted by trapped souls. He probably sold to a lot of desperate types. He probably wasn't used to somebody like Dolly.

Dolly went over the thing from bumper to bumper, crawled under it, leaned over the engine for I don't know how long. Guns and cars, those are Dolly's purview, and especially cars that have as little computer stuff in them as possible. If any. This one didn't have any, a retro rebuild on a modern Jeep chassis, maybe by whoever sold it or traded it to this used car guy. Maybe by somebody else. She added the lock boxes underneath after, aluminum to block wireless signals and scans. There's a couple of places where guns are hidden, I'm sure, and I wouldn't put it past her to have a sniper rifle broken down and stowed in the roll bars.

Does she actually have one stowed there? Did I help her do it? That seems likely.

When did she buy the Jeep? Where were we? We were getting ready for...

But it's gone again and I'm left looking at security protocols that look pretty much exactly like the protocols that I saw last year when we were fleeing...whoever...(probably the Russians, or an unnamed Russian agency) into the arms of whatever this unnamed American agency is. With all of those diamonds. Everybody wanted those diamonds, us included, I guess. More for the payday than anything else but I'd be shocked if Bristol didn't keep *any* to wear. It's so satisfying, to be proven right. But scary too, in this case, because these people have resources. Money and guns and personnel and helicopters. Contracts with us that were promptly broken. Whoops.

Null doesn't know where we're going, so they can't know, even if they have their guesses. I don't know where we're going, though I think maybe I do know. I think we went to one of these places. I think Dolly's been on this trail for awhile, and then I spent six months in VR, not realizing that something had gone terribly wrong. I think Dolly and Bristol put me there, hoping I'd be okay.

I pull off my headset like I'm breaking the surface of water after sitting at the bottom of a pool on a bet. I blink and look around. No time skip this time, I'm here and now. No headache, yet, though the flickers are still in my vision. "Are we there yet?" I ask before Dolly can ask how I am I'm tired of people having to ask me how I am.

"Five more minutes," Dolly says. Null laughs oddly.

"Are you okay?" I ask Null.

"Still not connecting," she says, gritting her teeth just a little. Sweating just a little. It's hot here, yeah, but she's panicking. I don't think we're going to hurt her. She's not on our side, I realize that now, but we're all on our own sides.

"So what's our game plan?" I ask because it's weird that we haven't talked about it. Or maybe we did when I was in a fugue state. "Just get in, grab whatever, get out? That's a little weird for us."

"It isn't our usual fare, no," Bristol doesn't turn around this time, I think she's playing with her phone. "There are some items in particular that can only be found at these sites. Or, found most easily at these sites. And we're in a particular position to find these locations."

"Gotcha," I say. Did we talk about the diamond heist in front of Null? Probably not. No reason to. Dolly has so many other things to brag about, that clusterfuck of an adventure doesn't need to be on the table.

"There's probably gonna be surveillance even," Dolly adds. "Bitsy, I think we packed your hoodie in that bag you got between your feet, Null..."

"What do I need?" Null says, and that's her biggest mistake; there isn't a single hacker who doesn't know about digital surveillance and what to do about it.

"I have a scarf she can borrow," Bristol says smoothly. "They take up so little room, I always have a bouquet of them in my purse nowadays."

"Thanks, I just wasn't ready for all of this," Null says in a rush.

"If we had the time, I'd take a look," I say and we both kind of shrug.

"Okay so there's probably gonna be a keycard lock, I should mention that," Dolly says.

"And do we have—" I know the answer.

"Nah, why would we?" Dolly grins, glances at me over her shoulder. "You can handle that." I can handle that, of course I can.

An overwhelming sense of déjà vu settles over me as we finish bumping down the green tunnel that was once a road and pull up to a tall chain link fence, the top of it still shiny in the daggers of sunlight that slice through the canopy. The grass is tall, hide-a-tiger tall, and the screaming of cicadas or crickets or whatever is louder, higher pitched. Dolly gets out with a set of bolt cutters that she was keeping God knows where and cuts the hank of chain that's keeping the gate closed and pushes it open. Bristol slides over and drives the Jeep through. I didn't know Bristol could drive stick. She's in riot gear too, and I guess for once didn't complain about doing it. She was so proud when she found those velvet combat boots. Null's just in jeans and a t-shirt, essentially. And the hoodie. Then I remember she's still got the ballistic vest Dolly loaned her and I'm relieved; then I remember she's one of the bad guys. Or rather, one of the not-us guys. We aren't really good, are we?

I take a deep breath, hold it a sec, let it out. Then we're all getting out of the Jeep. I've got my phone out and I'm looking around for the cameras.

The stuff for the keycard reader is in a flat pack toolkit in one of my cargo pockets and I practically sleepwalk through disarming it. It wants to send a signal to...somebody...to say that it's been accessed, and I cancel that. The cameras are probably motion sensors, probably recording and broadcasting any time there's any movement, but if this is a mothballed site, what's the likelihood of somebody having eyes on that feed 24/7? Proportional to how recent our last site visitation was. I don't have that information; I mean, I do. I was there and Dolly's told me over and over, but I've still got that block.

The door buzzes and kachunks open. I hum Dolly's little song as I slip inside and find a security panel a few steps down the hallway, flip it open and find a place to plug my headset into it, trusting Dolly and Bristol to come in and cover and all that. I remember doing this, in the other place, a weird overlay of memory and present action, and without thinking, punch in some numbers. The panel turns green, chimes gently, and I pull my headset up to watch the data stream by. Nobody's been here in a long time, not inside. Once a year, looks like, a walkthrough for infrastructure and security testing. Nobody assigned here. Just this level, two garages.

Bristol is talking and I think maybe Null is asking questions but their voices are kind of a smooth background murmur, no particular words sticking out as I find the code for the camera directives, find the memory banks where recorded activity is stored, and watch the last thirty minutes or so on 10x speed before wiping our arrival and looping a previous recording of some feral hogs trotting through the grass outside the fence. They must check the perimeter more often, with how often it storms, with the wildlife and the vigorous foliage. Nothing on schedule this week or even this month, though. And it is April. There's something about finding that out that steadies me.

Why would the same code work in two places? Personnel maybe. I look for an inventory sheet, forward it to Dolly and Bristol's phones. The code, the numbers are swimming in front of my eyes and I pull down my headset and see the hallway lit by its low energy backup lights, the way it was when we came in, and I see it lit only by our bouncing flashlight beams, the way it was at the other place. It was a different place, right, and not here? The not-gas station guy didn't look at all like he recognized us, unless he's set dressing, an actor, somebody Dolly knows from before we all got together. We don't hit the same place twice, that's stupid. We wouldn't steal the same diamonds twice, would we? Bristol might. We kind of did. I guess not; they never truly left our possession once we took ownership.

I stumble a little, over an uneven tile that isn't uneven when I look at it again, and Dolly catches me by the arm while looking at her phone. My head still hurts but I kind of don't care. I wonder why I never just keep my own bottle of pills around. The good stuff. Probably because VR wouldn't be my only bad habit then.

"This way, isn't it?" Bristol asks. Null seems to be keeping close to her. Maybe my one lucid non-tech thought of the day, I wonder if Null thinks that in a bind, she can take Bristol hostage and get herself out of here. That won't work out well for her. Dolly just nods, takes point, and I follow right behind her. I resist the impulse to hold onto her belt to steady myself;

I've done it a couple times, if we were on the move and I was using my VR goggles. It works well enough but isn't advisable. Add it to the list. This is still better than working at a convenience store, or getting an internship or whatever, and hoping to be allowed to have a life that's good enough, that I'm happy with.

Not all of the security measures are linked to that panel, that would be dumb, but many of them are linked to the motion sensors of the camera, which both sense that we're moving but don't see anything unusual, and so are super confused about whether everything is fine. Most of the stuff is just as simple as doors locking down, but they've got some weaponized drones too that we need to watch out for, either for me to hack or for somebody to baseball swing out of the air. Or shoot, I guess. I don't think any of us has a baseball bat. I don't have a baseball bat. Maybe Bristol should have a cricket bat or a field hockey stick or something. A blunt weapon, but make it classy.

"Where are you thinking, Bitsy?" Dolly asks.

"Me? I thought this was your rodeo."

"Oh, it is." Oh, I get it. She's just trying to keep me engaged.

"Physical records is down the hall."

"Good old fashioned paper files, gotta love that perfume right, Bristles?"

I can practically hear Bristol roll her eyes. She didn't put on perfume for this, I only just now noticed. "Old books is the perfume people like so much, Dolly, not manila envelopes and tiresome government records."

"Oh right right." Dolly opens a door apparently at random and I turn around because it's like I can *feel* Null cringing behind me. "Not the stairs."

"There are no stairs," I say, and then I cringe myself when I look because it is suddenly so bright, like we're outside again, but no, just a flood of natural light through skylights which are probably those transparent solar panels. I think the lifespan of those isn't great, so they're probably just normal windows again by now. There's a grid of drones parked on the floor, though, ready to take flight, but all still in standby, little red lights on them blinking to show they're fully charged.

Dolly looks at us and laughs. "Boo!" she says, and shakes her head, pulling the door shut. "They'll just stay sleepin', right Bitsy?"

"Right," I say, but I don't know why I'm so sure. Then I remember I fixed them to stay just sleeping, that's why.

If I stick this out, I'll know what happened. I'll be fine again.

We keep going.

This place isn't so big that it'll take a lot to go through. The stairs are lit by red backup lights that are actually kind of soothing for me, or at least don't make my head feel worse. Most of the rooms on this top floor really are decommissioned, just full of rolling chairs around fake wood conference tables, monitors that aren't plugged into anything, lockers all hanging open and empty, dry and dusty bathrooms.

Dolly turns a faucet handle and nothing happens, not even a rattle from the pipes. "Makes you wonder about their fire control," she says with a wink.

"They probably have condensed aerosol fire suppression, with all the tech that they had," I say. "Actually that's probably on its own server and backup generator so that if—"

"Bits, sweetie, she was making a joke," Bristol says, her hand on my shoulder. "Though non-water fire suppression is I'm sure *very interesting,* and we can talk about it another time."

"It is," I say. Normally this would be funny, me giving a detailed response to Dolly banter, but we're all tense, we all have our role, and I'm sure we're all hoping nobody misses her cue. Especially me.

Null can miss her cues I guess. She's probably missed a few already. They've probably got some kind of tracker on her. We didn't check that out, unless Dolly was just so sneaky that I didn't notice.

When we find the records room, it isn't much larger than a regular office but jam-packed with filing cabinets, and Dolly just starts rooting around. "I'd offer help, but..." Bristol trails off.

"It'd ruin your manicure," Dolly says, her grin flashing in the indistinct light. "Just gotta find the right...vector or year or whatever, and we're golden."

"Why is it paper?" Null asks, the first she's spoken in a really, really long time. Guess she didn't figure out how to get her internet back.

"You can't exactly remote hack a file cabinet," Dolly laughs.

"Yeah, but we're here and they left everything."

"Because who would *bother,*" Bristol asks, wrinkling her nose a little. If she had white gloves on, she'd be drawing lines in the dust all over the place and tsking. Dolly's still laughing, but more quietly than her typical bray, a file folder open on her forearm as she skims it. Except I feel like she's looking at a clipboard, and remember sunlight. A big door, with a separate lock. The smell of old rubber and engine grease.

"Did you find what you're looking for?" I ask. I feel like I'm aware of a ticking clock.

"Yup. Yes I did." She takes some of the papers, folds them in a square, jams them in a cargo pocket. She claps her hands together, making us all jump a little in the quiet. "Alrighty, on to looting, our favorite part!"

"Wait you're not going to—" Dolly takes my arm, leads me stumbling out of the room before I can finish.

"I'll explain as much as you want me to right now, but you gotta consider that's the difference between Null walkin' outta here and not," she says in my ear, barely louder than breathing. "Because she can't know what this says. That'll be the difference between you 'n' Bristol walkin' outta here or not."

Chapter Nineteen

"Where shall we 'loot'?" Bristol asks, quirking her lips a little, but I don't know what's funny. For some reason, everybody's looking at me.

"Um," I say, pulling up my headset, looking at the map. Maybe I will just hold Dolly's belt and let her walk me. The pressure of the straps make my head feel a little better. Or that pill is making me feel a little better. Or I don't know, the less I'm talking, the better. "Looks like this place is pretty much cleared out. Another drone room, and it does look like all the drones are nonlethal. Or they have been so far."

"Oh, they the kind with the little tasers?" Dolly asks.

"Yeah. And little onboard systems to dial for emergency. They're smart enough to tell the difference between intruder and fire and stuff." Dolly already knows. I scroll through more information but there's no way I can read enough while we're just standing here to truly understand where we are. Those empty rooms are labeled classrooms. There's more probably empty rooms labeled clinics. Isolation rooms. Drone rooms. Mess hall. Command. Garage. And...second garage? That's so *weird*.

Somebody, probably Dolly, starts walking me while I'm doing this, and I'm not really paying attention until Bristol says

"No, I will not" in such a tone that I pull the headset down again.

"What? What's wrong?"

"Dolly is disgusting, is what's wrong." Bristol is shaking her head, Null is just wide eyed and Dolly is grinning, eminently pleased. Her natural state. She's also holding some manner of military ration, still sealed by the looks of it, and not recently. Probably within the last fifteen years anyway.

"I just said that the date's still good," Dolly says with a shrug. "And wondered what the dessert was."

"You'd totally eat it," I say.

"Of course I would. It's food, ain't it?"

"It is not," Bristol says, and I remember her delight at that gourmet restaurant. And she's been to lots since; I guess it's easier for her to just pretend she's never been hungry than to remember anything from that time. I don't really blame her. I do wonder if anybody ended up paying that bill, though.

"Okay Bitsy, c'mon, where to?" Dolly asks. I blink; I don't know where she put the MRE and I don't remember when she lit a cigarette but I blink again and there's no cigarette. The MRE is still gone.

"The armory," I say. "Though I don't know if they left anything worth selling."

"Maybe they left a few museum pieces. Or the kind I'd like to add to my personal collection."

"Yeah maybe they have an early-aughts AR or something," I say.

"They never did start making those again," she says thoughtfully. "Probably for the better."

"That bad a gun?" Null asks.

"That bad for society, more like." Bristol may as well be tapping her foot and rolling her eyes. She isn't, but maybe she hears that ticking clock too. Honestly, she just hates spending time in dusty military holes. Who can blame her?

"This red light is creepy," Bristol says as we walk down the hallway. More déjà vu, she said this last time, or in the other place. Dolly's whistling that *song* again.

"It's so your night vision isn't fucked," Dolly says as she reaches for the next door. I get an overwhelming sense of dread, that movie theater impulse to yell.

"Don't go in there." I say it, but keep myself from yelling it. When's the last time I yelled anything?

"What's wrong?" Null sounds...relieved?

"Nothing this time," Dolly says, hand still on the door but paused to look at me. "There was last time, though."

"Last time?" Null says, but I'm not confused, finally. Things are clicking into place for me. Last time. Last time, the other one of these, Dolly didn't find what she was looking for in records. And then things started to go bad, to slide slowly sideways. I messed up hacking the inventory computer that they had, trying to figure out what was there besides the rifles and grenade launchers and prototype energy things, which we knew didn't work well and had a habit of failing spectacularly and we left alone. The security on the computer was twisty, it was more than a usual algorithm, and I tried it, flubbed it, tried it again and got it. But the damage was already done, I already felt off.

"Dolly, we need to talk about—" but she's already opening the door I didn't want her to open and I never pull my gun but I've pulled my gun again and—

Nothing happens.

Dolly looks so damn smug but I'm so relieved I don't even care. Bristol almost looks bored, and maybe she is bored, who can say. She probably would rather be catching up on her messages and planning her next party. What kind of payday are we even looking for here? And why would any of us need it?

"Not now, Bits. See, it's clear." Just dust on the floor, and dust on the empty shelves and racks. Dolly's right, there's nothing. She even walks around the room with her arms out while we watch her and nothing happens. But it makes me think of the active camo box, and that isn't in my pocket anymore. I don't know when that happened.

"I believe we ought to hurry more than this," Bristol says. "I'm certain Nicolai is in position by now."

"It might really help me if I knew what this was," Null says but kind of quietly, so we'd have the option to ignore her. "Especially if you already got what you needed, Dolly?"

"What, you don't like walking around places like this?" Dolly asks.

"Not particularly," Null says as we continue. Dolly looks at me and shrugs, like 'what's her problem' and I laugh because what else can I do.

It's like we're clearing the rooms in a video game level, just making sure we haven't missed anything. I almost expect to see ammunition and medpacks just on the floor when we go down the hallway to the final room, the thing that looked like a garage but not a garage on the map. So very irritating and inconvenient for whoever ran this program to not label their maps, but I guess they knew what the rooms were so why bother. Like how in the olden days in Britain there used to be three spices that got set out on the table, salt and pepper and something else, except nobody ever wrote down the something else because why would you? Everybody knew. I think about that sometimes. Salt and pepper and...Savory? Rosemary? I wonder what size the holes on the shakers were. Or if they were shakers. Didn't people use salt cellars for a really long time? A salt cellar and a pepper mill and—

There are footsteps in the hallway behind us except there aren't. It's just my memory overlap again, welling up, glitching in flashes. Us running, us with Null and nobody running, Dolly slapping a new magazine into her gun, Dolly's gun still holstered. Sparking drone parts scattering across the institutional tile floor, the smell of burnt electronics and gunfire.

There's another layer of security here, of course there is. Not a retinal scan (those are always a bitch to circumvent if you don't have a live eye with appropriate security clearance), just another keypad on its own circuit, not even as hard as the first one. Dolly probably could've just talked to it with a paperclip, the way some basic car computers can be adjusted. Funny how paperclips still exist.

Then the door buzzes and Dolly shoves it open and there's more light again, this time because part of the roof caved in under the weight of kudzu and neglect. There's so much sunlight after the dark hallways with their soothing red that for a second it feels like my eyes are just full of TV static and I think I might just fall down from another migraine right there like a cut-string puppet. But my eyes adjust, and the pain doesn't come again. It's just full of leaves and vines and grass in here, and we startle up a flock of black winged birds when we start to walk through.

I look around for shimmers in the air, expecting...what am I expecting? Active camo like the officer in Bristol's convoy had. But there's nothing. Why did we walk through this whole place if all Dolly wanted was a handful of papers from practically the first room we came to? But then I realize what we're walking past, what this whole garage is actually full of, and I stop and grab a handful of the vines, pull. Null actually gasps.

It's power armor, not huge bullshit anime style power armor that's tall as a building, but stuff a person could get in that would make them eight, nine feet tall. The edges don't make sense, all angular and weird, like those airplanes that are built to deflect radar. Imagine a unit of these, invisible to radar, marching onto a location. I stare into the dark mirror of the closed-face helmet that I just uncovered, remembering one with a shattered visor, with the arm sparking and broken, dripping hydraulic fluid and blood. I remember somebody's raw voice, Dolly's, yelling "God damn it Bits! What's wrong with you?!" I don't know what Bristol was doing. Finding our exit, I guess. I don't know how we got out, I can't remember how we got out, and what I remember now is my ringing ears and the smell of burning, snow that just wouldn't stop falling, no it's burning paper, maybe burning other things but there's no bullets flying anymore.

I pull off more of the vines like shucking a cob of corn, the suit shining in the sunlight, and I reach its power source. Nuclear, a surprise and not a surprise. Something like that isn't enough yield to go critical, but it doesn't mean that a bunch of them together didn't make a big enough boom all the same. Oh I can't take credit for that. That's what Bristol was doing, actually dirtying her hands with grenades or with C4 I can't remember which it was now, and it isn't important right this second. We, I, tripped the security; there were lots of automated turrets with lots of lethal rounds, and we blew up all of those suits of armor and dragged ourselves away from the smoking aftermath before human personnel arrived.

We went there looking for the papers, the physical files, that pertained to Dolly's defunct super soldier program, and hoped to also have something to sell in the process because old habits, right? What we got was a hurt Dolly—a very badly hurt Dolly—and a very messed up me. Hypnosis as a thought-virus, I guess I should've learned more, sooner, about brainhacking. And it's a good thing we sold all those diamonds plus stole that government money last year, because cybernetic arms still cost a lot, especially ones that just look like normal.

I blink to reset, look around. Bristol isn't actually bored, that's just the cultivated look on her face, so her actual watchfulness isn't apparent. Dolly's leaning against a non-kudzu'd wall with her arms crossed and an unlit cigarette hung on her lip. And Null is just standing there, watching, waiting, so expectant she's ready to come out of her skin. "Why are we all just standing here?" she asks. I don't really have a good answer for her.

"Will these work?" I ask Dolly, even as I put my hand on one and feel it humming, faintly.

"They will. But we're not doing anything with 'em right now, that's Nicky's job."

"So that's it? You just came here for some papers and you're going to leave?" Null's voice cracks just a little and I can't tell if she's upset, in disbelief, or what.

"Sure are. Call it disaster tourism," Dolly says cheerfully. "We ready to roll?" she asks me.

"I think so." The papers. The hypnosis. There's a phrase that makes it so Dolly doesn't feel pain, a phrase that makes it so Dolly will kill targets indiscriminately. It took a lot for me to decrypt the map of the sites in the first place. There's more, and none of those phrases were ever stored electronically. But Dolly is Dolly and wants to stay that way. I wouldn't have her any other way, though I think Bristol might not mind having some level of control.

But Null. Dolly hits the big red button that opens the garage door and we walk out to the Jeep, Null right there with us. Then it's just me and Bristol and Null, and I don't know where Dolly is. The last time we had to shake a government asset, Bristol kissed him with special lipstick and we just kind of left him at an abandoned bus station. None of us are really in a kissing position here. Null is messing with her equipment when her phone rings and she startles, drops it.

The gunfire comes from nowhere, a shimmer in the air that I only just barely see, the muzzle flashes interrupting it. Null kind of shudders backwards and then collapses with a coughing wheeze and in the held-breath post-gunshot silence, even the bugs quiet, I can still hear her breathing. I expect it to stop every time I hear her take a breath and then I notice the rubber bullets on the ground. Oh. Her phone stops ringing and the pause is too quiet, all those screaming bugs silent. Then the phone rings again.

"I know, I know, we just keep leaving witnesses but," Dolly shrugs. "C'mon, we gotta go."

"You just had to be so *dramatic* about it," Bristol says.

"Like you're one to talk. And I wanted to use the camo thingie."

"We're going to have incoming," I say, once I feel like I've caught my breath. "And we'll have to ditch the Jeep."

Dolly shakes her head. "I really liked that Jeep."

Epilogue

I've got about a million messages that I'm skimming to make sure they're okay to delete. Lots of spam, there's always lots of spam, but there's listservs and group chats and newsletters and all the digital detritus that just piles up if you're not on top of it. And I wasn't keeping good track for...awhile, even after Dolly came and got me. I didn't realize I wasn't, and I also apparently didn't spend six months in immersion, but I thought that was the truth when I said it to Dolly. It wasn't six months but it was still...awhile.

I wonder now if my real estate guy actually said anything about there being tigers, or if my brain mashed up Pablo Escobar's hippos with military tiger teams. I don't ask him about it when I message him to clean the villa out and put it on the market. From what I can tell, nobody ever went there. Probably nobody was ever even able to trace me, but I don't want to visit and find out.

Sometimes I still catch myself whistling that little scrap of hypnosis song; it's the kind meant to help you focus, and even though I wasn't conditioned the way Dolly was during her super soldier program, it helps. And of course it makes me think of Dolly and her deconditioning, and the look on her face when the kill command words didn't work anymore. That's about as far into brainhacking as I'm ever going to get, and having been brainhacked once, I can say I'm not interested in revisiting the situation ever again.

Eventually, I reach inbox zero and pull off my VR headset. I have a plane to catch.

Jennifer R. Donohue grew up at the Jersey Shore and now lives in central New York with her husband and their Doberman. Though she got a bachelor's degree in psychology, she has always wanted to write. She currently works at her local public library, where she also facilitates a writing workshop. Her work has appeared in Daily Science Fiction, Syntax & Salt, Escape Pod, Truancy, DreamForge and elsewhere. She blogs at Authorized Musings, where she shares fiction and the tribulations of the writing life, and tweets @AuthorizedMusin.